Dear Brio Girl,

Have you ever felt uneasy about sharing your faith? If so, maybe it's because you've assumed the only way to talk about God is with words.

You'll love getting to know Jacie. She's a cool teen girl—just like you—who learns to share her faith without words. I think the two of you will really click!

Let me know what you think when you've finished her story, okay?

Your Friend,

Susie Shellenberger, BRIO Editor
www.briomag.com

Brio Girls

from Focus on the Family®
and
Bethany House Publishers

brio girls

REAL Faith MEETS REAL Life

Hannah   Solona   Tyler   Becca

Stuck in the Sky

Created • Written by
LISSA HALLS JOHNSON

BETHANYHOUSE
MINNEAPOLIS, MINNESOTA

Focus on the Family books are available at special quantity discounts when purchased in bulk by corporations, organizations, churches, or groups. Special imprints, messages, and excerpts can be produced to meet your needs. For more information, contact: Resource Sales Group, Focus on the Family, 8605 Explorer Drive, Colorado Springs, CO 80920; or phone (800) 932-9123.

A Focus on the Family book published by
Bethany House Publishers
A Ministry of Bethany Fellowship International
11400 Hampshire Avenue South
Bloomington, Minnesota 55438
www.bethanyhouse.com

Printed in the United States of America by
Bethany Press International, Bloomington, Minnesota 55438

Library of Congress Cataloging-in-Publication Data

Johnson, Lissa Halls, 1955–
    Stuck in the sky / by Lissa Halls Johnson
        p. cm. — (Brio girls)
Summary: Jacie experiences conflicting feelings about her Christian faith, pursuing her interest in art, and the "hot" new boy at school.
    ISBN 1-56179-951-3
[1. Christian life—Fiction. 2. Friendship—Fiction. 3. Schools—Fiction.]
I. Title. II. Series.
    PZ7.J63253 St 2001
    [Fic]—dc21

                                             2001002560

For my daughter, Misty
the Sunshine girl

Thank you for sharing
my biggest life adventure.
I couldn't have done it
without you.

LISSA HALLS JOHNSON is a fiction writer for Focus on the Family. Previously a member of the ADVENTURES IN ODYSSEY creative team, she is the author of fourteen novels for teens and young readers.

chapter 1

September 5—First Day of School—Ugh!

It's not that I don't like school. It's okay. It's where I get to see my friends every day. It's just that the first day is always miserable.

I'll be leaving for school in a few minutes. And I'm hoping this year will be my art break-through. I've been stuck for so long. Maybe my art teacher, Mrs. Waisanen, will be able to help.

My biggest frustration is this: I wish I knew how to capture the soul of a person on paper or canvas. I wish I knew how to make them come alive the way I see them, not just how the eye sees them. I've seen portraits and *landscapes that are technically correct, but lack magic. I've seen others that capture my attention so well that I can't NOT look at them. I'm held, spell-bound by something deeper.*

I want to draw like that. Paint like that. But it seems so out of my grasp.

"Come in!" Jacie called absently in response to the giggles and laughter outside the shack she used as her art studio. Her mind was elsewhere—still absorbed in her journal-thoughts.

"We can't!" Becca called. "It's locked."

Jacie put her journal down and swiveled the overstuffed rocker around to face the shed door. She shook herself back into the real world. Standing, she unlatched the door and threw it open. "Hi, you guys!" Her bright sunshine smile lit up her face. She loved seeing her friends—anytime, anywhere. And *here* was always the best.

Solana was in the process of pulling a scrunchie from her long, dark brown hair. "What in the world are you doing locking your door?" Solana asked. "Are you afraid some weirdo is going to come steal your paints?" She moved her head and her hair fell past her shoulders, almost to her waist.

"It was the wind," Jacie answered. She plopped her backside into the chair. She lifted her sketchbook and pencil, and prepared to focus on the page. Sometimes just having her friends around helped her draw. They seemed to distract her enough to let her hand move more quickly. She always liked to see what came out of her when her friends were around. She glanced at them for inspiration.

Becca and Solana looked at each other, then outside.

"*What* wind?" Becca asked Solana.

"Too many paint fumes are melting her brain," Solana said. She adjusted her leather skirt, twisting it around her hips until the seams lined up just right.

Becca shook her head, her thick brunette ponytail swishing back and forth. "We always knew the poor girl was more than a nugget short of a Happy Meal."

Jacie tried holding back a smile at their teasing. "Wind comes with thunderstorms. You know we've had a lot of them lately."

"Every day," Becca agreed.

"In the *afternoon*," reminded Solana. "This is *morning*."

Jacie felt stumped. Why *had* she locked the door? She wasn't stupid, but sometimes when she got involved in journaling or writing, her brain switched to another time zone—or another dimension. Maybe it was the land of dementia where her grandfather occasionally visited.

"Like my new shorts?" Becca interrupted to ask Jacie, pretending to model them. "I can't believe my mother actually picked a good style. And the right size, too."

Jacie took in the khaki hiker's shorts with pockets all over them. Becca was an athlete with an athletic build. She preferred wearing clothes she could be active in rather than girl-clothes like Jacie preferred. "They certainly suit you."

Becca looked at Solana. "That means she doesn't like them."

"Yes, I do," Jacie protested.

"But you wouldn't wear them," Becca retorted.

"Would you wear *this* dress?" Jacie shot back, jumping from the chair and twirling around to show off her new cotton dress, a white tank underneath.

"No," Becca answered.

"Okay, then." Jacie turned to Solana, scanning her up and down. "Feeling your *Chola* roots today?" she asked, pointing to Solana's lips. On some days Solana loved dressing with full *Latina Chola* makeup to be sure everyone knew her Hispanic roots—as if they couldn't tell without it.

"Now why would you ask that?" Solana said, with a smile that said she knew exactly what she was doing.

"Black lipstick. Heavy eye makeup. That's an awful lot of blue eye shadow, isn't it?"

Solana shrugged. "It's the first day. I've got to make an impression."

Jacie turned to Becca. "You notice she didn't say she wanted to make a *good* impression?"

Solana laughed. "Attention. It's all about attention."

Jacie wished she felt as comfortable with her body and heritage as her friends did. She was never quite sure how people would react if they knew her absent father was African-American. Although she looked as though she were biracial, since her mother was white, most people didn't ask questions. She loved her dad a lot. But who *she* was, she wasn't sure.

Jacie looked at her friends. "So what brought you guys here so early?"

"Reality check: Have you forgotten already?" Becca asked. She looked at Solana. "She really *is* losing it."

"No more than usual," Solana told her. She looked at Jacie. "Registration, Paintasauraus," Solana said. "Mr. Girard must be wondering where you are."

Jacie looked at her little wind-up clock sitting on a garage-sale dresser. "I'm late!"

"Yeah!" Solana snorted. "Forgot to set your alarm again."

"But we knew that was probably the case," Becca said. "So! As always, your *Brio* friends have come to rescue you." She threw her arms out with such force, her triple-chain necklaces clinked the dog tags at the end of them.

"But without Tyler, the group rescue is not complete," Jacie said. "Where is he, anyway?"

"Getting us coffee and hot chocolate from Copperchino," Becca said. "A kind of first-day-of-school party."

"Well, let's go, then," Jacie said.

"Oh! I almost forgot," Solana said, reaching into her tiny shoulder purse and bringing out a crumpled brochure. She handed it to Jacie. "This sounded like something you should look at. I found it at the library." Solana rolled her eyes. "It's not like I can use it. I can't draw a stick figure worth looking at."

Jacie took it from her and opened it. She scanned the pages.

Art Mentoring Institute's
National Art Conference
Learn from the Masters

"I can't believe it!" Jacie shrieked. "Look at this! They match you with an artist and you get this intense art training with them for an entire week!" She read the names of the mentors out loud. "Can you believe this? This is absolutely incredible."

"Um," Becca said, "Maybe we should be impressed?"

"Yes, you should be impressed," Jacie said. "It's like Michael Jordan coaching your girls' basketball team."

Becca's eyebrows shot up. "That'd be pretty amazing."

Jacie tugged playfully on Solana's hair. "Or like some famous laboratory taking you in and giving you intense one-on-one for a week just to give you a better grasp of nuclear physics."

A faraway look crossed Solana's brown eyes. "That would be the most incredible experience of my life."

"These artists aren't nobodies. I know who they are. They're the best." Jacie tucked a stray curl behind her ear. "Some of my favorite African-American artists are here, too. Annie Lee, Kenneth Gatewood, Melinda Byers. I would *love* to study under them." She read further and gasped. "Look at the seminars that will be offered!"

"Oh, yeah, like I know what they are," Solana said.

Jacie started to dance around the room, still reading the brochure out loud. Her black curly hair jiggled about her face. Inside her head, all she could think about was the journal entry she had just written. *Could this be my answer? Could I really learn to be a true artist?*

Solana grabbed Jacie's sleeve, stopping her in mid-flight. "Come on, *Loca*, we gotta get outta here."

"Wait!" Jacie flipped the brochure over, unwilling to let go of it. Her eyes flashed to the dates. "This sounds like it's probably right around Spring Break," she said her voice picking up more excitement. "This would be INCREDIBLE! I'd be spending one-on-one time with someone who could really help me."

Mrs. Waisanen, her art teacher, had helped her as much as she could over the past couple of years. *But she isn't a professional. She always complains that she can't keep up with me. And now there would be someone who wouldn't have to keep up. They'd be so far ahead.* She tried pulling away from Solana to dance away more of her exhilaration.

Becca was flipping through Jacie's sketchbook, oblivious to her little dance. But Jacie didn't care. No one would understand how incredible this would be. *No one but Dad and he's not even here.*

Jacie finally shook Solana loose and read the next lines. Instantly, the dance stopped. *It figures.* There was nothing to dance about. *I should have known something this good couldn't happen to me.* She marched over to the trash basket and dropped it in. "Come on, let's go," Jacie said, grabbing her backpack. "Mr. Girard's going to kill me."

"It's okay," Becca said, glancing up from the sketchbook. "He'll only kill you *after* you help out with the registration. By the way, Jace, I really like this sketch of the horses."

"What did you just do?" Solana demanded.

"Uh, nothing," Becca said. "Don't you want to see this sketch of the horses?"

"Not you, goof. *Her.*"

"What'd she do?"

"Threw away the brochure I gave her."

Becca jumped up from the chair. "What'd you do that for?"

"You guys aren't very nice," Jacie said. "You get me all excited when you know I can't go to something like that." She opened the shack door and motioned for them to follow her out.

"Why can't you go to the conference?" Solana asked.

"Like I have $1,500 for the tuition, plus coming up with airfare from Denver to Atlanta."

Solana passed Jacie going out the door. "I'm sorry. I didn't even think—"

"I wish you would have, Solana," Jacie retorted.

"I just saw *ART* and I thought of you, that's all," Solana said.

Jacie closed her shed door and turned the key in the lock. She sighed, the initial anger dissipating quickly like it always did. "I know."

Becca marched over to Jacie's car. "Shotgun!" she called.

Jacie looked around outside, confused. "How'd you guys *get* here? You certainly didn't walk—" She looked pointedly at Solana who never walked anywhere if she didn't have to.

"My mom dropped us off," Becca said. "She had to take Alvaro to the hospital in Denver."

Jacie cringed. "More burn treatments?"

"Yeah."

"Poor little guy." Jacie ached for Becca's foster brother. Becca's family had taken in a young Guatemalan boy who had been severely burned in a fire that took the life of his mother. Without treatment in the States, he probably would have been severely scarred, or infection would have set in and he could have died.

"We knew you'd take us to school," Solana said.

"Am I your taxi?" Jacie asked, one dark brow raised.

"You are now that you're the only one with a car," Solana said.

"Great," Jacie teased as she opened the door to her metallic green Toyota Tercel. "Just what I wanted this morning after that little stunt—to spend more time with you two."

"Get in," Solana said to Becca.

"I already claimed shotgun!" Becca said.

"I'm not crawling into that back seat," Solana complained while Becca held the seat bent forward for her.

"Tough. I have longer legs than you."

"I have a bigger behind than you. If I bend over to get in, it will shock the world with its immensity."

"You don't have a big rear end," Becca laughed. "No one can see you anyway. Just get in."

"Come on, you guys, or I'm leaving you both here," Jacie said. Her heart felt heavy, but she knew she had to leave the idea of the art conference where it was—in the trash. Since there was no way to do anything about it, she might as well focus on the first day of school.

Her *junior* year. How cool was that? She forced a smile that she didn't feel.

Solana stuck her tongue out at Becca. As she settled into the back seat, she said, "Move the seat up."

"Let me get in first." Becca threw her backpack on the floor as she settled into the pale green seat. She reached down and slid the seat forward. "Is that enough for Your Immenseness?"

Solana poked her head between the seats. "No. I need another three feet. I'm so huge, I simply won't last a moment wedged into this tiny place. Why don't we switch places?"

"You aren't big. Dream on, *Chica*."

Solana peered at Jacie. "It's so weird that the poorest one of all of us is the only one with a car," she said. "I guess it helps to have an absent father who's trying to score points."

"That's so mean," Becca said.

Jacie laughed as she started the car and threw it into reverse. "But it's so true," she said. The car hiccuped backward.

"Can't you drive this thing yet?" Becca squealed. "You've had it what—two weeks?"

"Ten days."

"I'm going to throw up," Solana threatened.

"You are not," Jacie said, shoving the stick into first. The car lurched forward. "I'm getting the hang of it. I'm only stalling on hills now."

"What are we going to do this year?" Becca asked. "We've got to make plans."

Solana groaned. "Oh no, not Becca the Organizer."

"We've got to decide important things, Sol. Like where we are going to meet for lunch. What changes we're going to make for the year. You know, like New Year's resolutions—only for school. Are we finally going to start a Bible study for other *Brio* readers? When do we start? Who do we invite? And when are you all going to join me at the Outreach Community Center?"

Jacie smiled. Becca had been trying to get the group of friends to join her as she helped feed the poor and homeless at the Outreach

Community Center for a long time. It wasn't that they didn't want to. It just hadn't worked out yet.

"We've got lots and lots of things to decide," Becca continued, moving constantly in her seat. She needed the seat belt to hold her in place all the time. "We've got to get moving on this stuff."

"Decide without me," Solana said. "You guys don't care what I think anyway." She plucked dark lipstick from her small purse hanging at her side. She leaned between the seats and yanked the rearview mirror down.

"Solana!" Jacie cried. "How do you expect me to drive?"

Solana applied the lipstick, then smushed her lips together. She checked her teeth for smudges, then sat back into her seat. "Okay, you can have it back now."

"We'd care more about how you feel, Solana," Becca said, "but since you always say the same thing, we're sick of hearing it and—"

"And you guys *don't* say the same things?" Solana asked. "You're always talking about God and the Bible and what's right and other stuff like that."

"It's not 'stuff,'" Becca said. "It's truth. And there's only one truth."

"According to you," Solana said. She stared out the window.

"Hey, guys, quit," Jacie said. "We're in this thing together."

"Since when?" Solana asked.

"Since fourth grade," Jacie said, not doing a great job at leaving the stop sign smoothly. She slammed the clutch back in and tried again. It wasn't much smoother, but it didn't get close to stalling.

"Can you please learn to drive this thing soon?" Solana muttered, clutching Becca's seat.

Jacie wished she didn't have to play referee for yet another fight between her friends. She wanted to be alone to make her own plans about how she could get past this plateau she had with her art. There was something missing, but she couldn't figure out what it was. It was like her true artist self was locked up inside her, screaming to get out, but she couldn't find the key. She looked for it in the work of other artists she admired. She looked for it in the art masters. She looked for it in what every artist seemed to tell her—paint or draw *every* day. But no matter what she did, nothing seemed to get her past the point where she was right now—where she'd been for the past six months. *Is there such a thing as artist's block?* she wondered. She intended to ask Mrs. Waisanen today after school. Maybe her art teacher would be able to help her. Jacie needed a plan and a program, and she was determined to get one that worked.

Jacie looked at her friends. Becca stared out her window. Solana slumped in the back seat, arms crossed. She knew their argument wouldn't last long. Over the past seven years, they'd been in more fights than Jacie could count, but they were still best friends. Jacie smiled at the thought. *We are so different! If we were to have just met today, I bet we wouldn't even be friends. It's the past—Alyeria—that connects us.*

Through the years, as Jacie and Becca grew in their faith, they still loved Solana and kept her close—hoping their lives and words would be a witness to her. They couldn't dump her just because she wasn't a Christian. They prayed together enough about Solana to know God wanted them to keep her as their friend. It certainly wasn't like Solana was a project. They loved her a lot, even if they couldn't understand why she didn't join them in their faith.

As Jacie shifted into third gear she took on her traditional role as the peacemaker. "Okay, you guys. Listen. Just think of it—we're juniors. *JUNIORS.* We're almost at the top! I don't know about you guys, but I'm not going to start off my junior year depressed. Let's count our blessings." *Being cheesy always distracts them from a dumb argument.* Jacie grinned.

Solana groaned.

"I still think we should decide what we're going to do and when we're going to do it," Becca insisted.

"Okay," Solana said, popping forward between the seats. "I'm going to add a minimum of three guys to my kissing list, and I hope to do this before Thanksgiving."

"Do horses count?" Becca asked.

All three girls broke into laughter. They all knew Solana was mostly talk. She did, however, fall for every guy that came along—especially the cute ones. If she ever had a boyfriend for longer than three weeks, they'd all pass out from shock.

"For you and Jacie, *any* male counts," Solana said. "Since neither of you have really grasped the concept of how wonderful kissing can be."

"We don't want to grasp that concept just yet," Becca said.

"I know, I know," Solana teased. "You're both saving your lips for marriage."

"Not quite that drastic," Becca replied. "But we did have a pact."

"What pact?" Solana asked. "Why wasn't I told about this?"

Becca turned around in her seat and peered around the headrest at Solana. "We made a promise that we would focus on our relationship with God for the summer."

"Oh, and you can't pay any attention to God if you have a guy in your life?" Solana asked. "Don't be stupid."

"Guys are distracting, okay?" Becca said. She turned back around and stared out the front window.

Jacie bit the inside of her lip. *I think I'd like to be distracted sometimes.*

"Guys are fun," Solana insisted. "They put spice into your life. Without guys where would we be?"

"We've got Tyler," Becca said. "We have guy input. Guy hugs. We don't need the added distraction of wondering if he'll kiss us, or ask us out or call us. Tyler is all the male input we need right now. Tyler and God."

I know I should agree with her, Jacie thought, trying to focus on the road ahead. *But sometimes I just wish I had a guy to talk to. To hold hands with. Someone who makes me feel special. Is it really wrong to want that? Or is it only wrong to do it the way Solana does—as if guys are disposable?*

Solana frowned. She crossed her arms and flopped back into her seat. "You guys are no fun. I don't even know why I hang out with you."

Jacie felt bad. Here she was internally siding with Solana, who snubbed God at every turn—instead of Becca, who was her spiritual sister. Shouldn't she always side with a Christian over a non-Christian?

Solana's voice brightened. "What about Tyler's buddy, Nate Visser? Haven't you had your eye on him?"

Jacie glanced at Becca whose cheeks looked like they were turning a bit red. *Bingo!* Solana hit a nerve.

"You know—"

"Watch out!" Becca yelled.

chapter 2

Jacie slammed on the brakes and cranked the steering wheel to the right, running off the road into the dirt. Her heart instantly started running fast.

Becca slammed her foot to the floor and braced her arm against the dash.

"YOU STUPID IDIOT!" Solana yelled at the motorcyclist that had cut in front of them as he turned into the school. He lifted his head as he went by, looking straight into the car, his bleached hair ruffled by the wind.

"Oh," Solana said quickly. "I take that back. He's cute!" She rolled down her window and screamed. "HEY! COME BACK!"

"Solana!" Jacie said, steering the car back onto the road. "Quit it. You're going to make me have an accident."

"ME? What about that jerk who just cut you off?"

"He couldn't help it," Becca defended. "The rise in the hill blocked his vision."

"*Blocked* his vision?" Solana parroted. "How would *you* know?"

"She's right," Jacie said. "I couldn't see him, so I guess he couldn't see me."

"Jerk or no jerk, he looked awfully cute," Solana said again, flip-flopping, as usual, when it came to guys. She always seemed torn between falling for a cute guy and being annoyed by his immature actions. "Black leather jacket," she sighed. "I love leather jackets on a guy."

"You like anything on a guy," Becca said.

Jacie turned into the school driveway. The cyclist revved the motor, zipped through the parking lot, and zoomed toward the rear of the school. Jacie parked her car in the nearest space. The girls piled out.

"You go find Mr. Girard and be Stony Brook High's official Welcome Wagon," Solana said to Jacie. "We're going to be lazy and sit in the Quad. No sense in starting school too early."

Jacie walked the length of the front of the school, passing the auditorium, offices, and pool. She loved her school. It was the newest one in Copper Ridge. The triangular architecture fit the cleft of the mountains into which the school was tucked. The builders had cut as few trees as possible, leaving an abundance of aspens, sycamores, and a variety of pines to surround the buildings. Stony Brook ran past the school, separating the gym and the football field. In the spring it was loud, full, and gushing. Now it ran slower, more like what she always thought of when a book described a brook as "babbling."

As she approached the gym, Jacie saw a tall girl wandering around, looking up at the building as though she'd never seen one before. She had thick, blond hair to her waist that was held back with plain, black clips. A perfect figure. It wasn't like Jacie always looked at figures, but some females seemed to be just so perfect that you couldn't help noticing. And this girl was certainly one of those. She would have been incredibly beautiful except for one thing—her clothes. She looked as though she'd just walked out of a fashion magazine—for farm wives.

"Hi," Jacie called out to her. "Can I help you?"

The girl was startled, as though Jacie had appeared with a gun instead of a friendly greeting. After a second of looking Jacie over, the girl seemed to relax. "I need to register," she said as Jacie continued to approach her.

"Come with me," Jacie told her, flashing her trademark smile. "I'm on my way there." Jacie had never been the new kid at school. But being anywhere new made her nervous and withdrawn.

The girl fell into step, but still seemed to be apprehensive. She held her shoulders in, her hands clasped tightly in front of her. It made Jacie think of an animal trying to look smaller.

"I'm Jacie." She wanted to put her arms around her and let her know everything would be okay. She hoped her words and kindness would accomplish almost the same thing.

"I'm Hannah," the girl said while continuing to look around.

"So, you're new here," Jacie said, trying to start a conversation and make this girl feel more at ease.

Hannah nodded.

"Where are you from?"

"Niles. It's a small town in Michigan." She stared down as if watching her brown, practical lace-up shoes move along the sidewalk.

"When did you move here?"

Hannah sighed deeply. "June."

"June? I'm surprised I haven't seen you around."

Hannah looked at Jacie and squinted against the sun. She opened her mouth to say something and then closed it. Jacie got a chance to finally look Hannah full in the face. No makeup. Perfect full lips without gloss or lipstick. Blue, blue eyes. The guys were really going to fall for this one.

Even Tyler? Jacie stifled a sigh. *Yes, especially Tyler.* It seemed to Jacie that *all* guys wanted tall blondes, not curly-haired brunettes of mixed ethnicity.

She shoved her thoughts aside. Reaching for the gym door, she yanked hard to open it. Noise spilled out. Students were everywhere—standing in lines, milling about, and talking in clumps. Hannah froze, her large, blue eyes opening wide.

"I'll stay with you if you like," Jacie said.

Hannah nodded. "I'm sorry," she said. "It's just that . . ." She said nothing more, her eyes still taking in the chaos inside.

"What grade are you?" Jacie asked.

"Eleven."

Jacie raised an eyebrow. No one said they were in eleventh grade. They liked being called *juniors*. "Okay, Hannah. We'll start over there with Mr. Girard. He's very funny. He's the Junior V.P. He's got this boyish, devilish side that cracks us up. He's kinda cute, actually."

Hannah nodded. "I can do this," she said, pulling herself to her full height. She looked at Jacie, her gaze strong and firm, unafraid. "I'm not usually like this. Really."

"I understand," Jacie reassured her. "New schools can be intimidating."

The girls stopped in front of a long folding table. A mid-sized man, Mr. Girard sported fashionable wire glasses. His face wore an impish grin that seemed like it might be hiding something. He sat behind the table, two cardboard boxes acting as file holders in front of him. "Jacie! Who have you found here? Looks like a new student."

"This is Hannah, Mr. Girard."

Mr. Girard wore his teasing smile as he addressed Hannah. "Didn't you once have a tail and fins?"

Hannah looked at him, confused. "I'm sorry?"

"Didn't I see you in the movie, *Splash?*"

Hannah shook her head. "I don't watch movies," she said simply.

Mr. Girard's smile vanished. He looked embarrassed. "Well, okay. I apologize. I just thought you looked like the actress, Daryl Hannah, and since you share the same name . . . well. We'll just dive right into business then. What school are you transferring from?" Mr. Girard asked, letting the friendly smile return to his face. "Do you have your records from there?"

"I've only been homeschooled," Hannah said, handing over a stack of papers.

Jacie tried not to stare. "You've never been to any school before?" she blurted. "No wonder you're so nervous." Jacie had lots of friends who had been homeschooled in their primary years. But she didn't know anyone who was still being homeschooled during high school.

"This is very different for me," Hannah agreed. "But I've had a great education." Her voice took on a strength and conviction Jacie hadn't yet heard in her. The girl seemed to transform before her eyes.

"My parents believe that being homeschooled provides a better education than public schools. They also feel Christian values are the most valuable traits to teach, and they knew they couldn't rely on anyone else to teach their values."

Wow. Sounds good to me. She sure comes out of her shell and has backbone for the things she believes in.

"That sounds very honorable," Mr. Girard said. "So why are you here now?"

The air seemed to go out of Hannah. "My mother is unable to teach advanced sciences and math. So here I am. No offense to you people or anything, but I really didn't want to attend public school."

Jacie instantly wanted to help her. To take her in and make everything okay. *I'll introduce her to Solana, Becca, and Tyler. She can be our new friend.* "It'll be okay," Jacie told her. "I've got just the person for you to meet—my friend Solana. She loves science. We also have a great chemistry teacher. Her name is Miss T. Amber. She likes being called Miss T. And no one knows what the T stands for." Jacie turned to Mr. Girard and smiled. "Can you get her into Miss T's class?"

Mr. Girard responded to Jacie's smile. "Anything for you, Jacie." Then his smile faded. "By the way, I need to talk to you about something before you leave."

Jacie's heart skipped a beat. Was he angry that she was late? Had she done something else wrong?

For several minutes, Mr. Girard and Hannah discussed Hannah's previous education so he could decide which classes she would need to graduate. Jacie looked around at the other students, wondering what in the world Mr. Girard had to say. When they were done, Hannah turned to Jacie.

"Can you show me where I need to go?" Hannah asked.

"Of course," Jacie said, giving her a big smile. "That's my job."

She paused and looked at the administrator. "What did you need to tell me, Mr. Girard?"

Hannah moved away, clutching her notebook to her chest.

Mr. Girard looked down at the table a moment, forming his thoughts. "I have bad news for you, Jacie."

Jacie looked at him, worried.

"You know our Beginning Art teacher left last June," he started.

"Yeah."

"Then two weeks ago Mrs. Waisanen had to leave town suddenly due to an illness in her family."

Jacie felt a funny flutter in her stomach. "Oh, no. How horrible! Will she still be able to teach?"

"Not for some time."

Jacie tried to look on the bright side. *This could be a good thing, couldn't it? Maybe even an answer to my prayer. The new art teacher might be able to help me with my problem.* She looked hopefully at Mr. Girard.

"Well, there's more. Due to budget cuts, we could only fill one of those positions. A Mr. Cornwall has taken that position."

"Is he good?" Jacie asked. She watched Hannah shrink away from the crowd of students, backing behind a cardboard sign.

"It doesn't matter if he's good," Mr. Girard said.

Jacie raised her eyebrow and cocked her head. "Why?"

"Because you aren't in the class."

Jacie felt sick to her stomach. "How could I not be in the art class?"

"With only one art teacher, there's no room."

"But it's *me*. I mean, it's not like I'm somebody special, but art is my *life*. It's who I am. It's how I express myself. I can't live without art. You know that."

"I know, Jacie. Believe me, I know. But there simply is no room. We have so many kids who *must* take a fine art for graduation credits that there isn't room for students such as you who simply want to improve."

Jacie opened her mouth to say something, but she couldn't think of what that would be.

"I'm really sorry."

"Is there a waiting list? Can I get on it?"

"The waiting list is long enough that I don't know that it would do you any good."

Hannah stood behind Mr. Girard, looking as though her ears had perked up. She watched Jacie with an odd interest. Jacie wished she would go away.

"I've got to do *some*thing."

"My hands are tied."

Jacie couldn't believe it. Her mother couldn't afford private art lessons. Her mother barely made enough money for the two of them to live on. They depended on the school to guide, critique, and teach.

"You'd better take Hannah and show her around," Mr. Girard said. "Come back when you're done. I'm sure there will be other students who will need your help."

Jacie nodded and turned to Hannah. In a subdued voice she said, "Come on, Hannah. Let's go."

chapter **3**

"It's going to be okay—I mean about the art class," Hannah said as Jacie led her from the gym. "All things work out for the best."

The verse Hannah referred to—Romans 8:28—zipped through Jacie's mind. *All things work together for good.* "Yeah, I guess," she said, not feeling it or believing it at all.

Jacie felt Hannah's hand on her arm—a soft, encouraging touch. "No need to be upset about it."

"Thanks," Jacie said. *But I am upset. Without art, I'm lost.* Not knowing what else to say to Hannah, she changed the subject. "Did you like being homeschooled?"

"I loved it," Hannah said, her shyness disappearing once again. "It was so fun learning about life and truth and God and the Bible all tied in with reading, sciences, and math. My mom would think up some very clever ways to integrate real life with our lessons. And we got to go on field trips to Chicago all the time. We went to museums and toured factories and lots of other places. Learning was rarely sitting at a table for hours. It was *doing* things. I'm convinced that I learned things on a much deeper level by being homeschooled. I also really respect my mom and her intelligence. It was fun, too, as I have grown up—I'm the oldest—to teach my younger siblings. That also helped me solidify what I learned. As a Christian family, we feel it's the best way to learn about what we believe and cement it into our hearts."

"You're right, it sounds great," Jacie said, meaning it. Jacie liked this girl's obvious strength about her convictions—when she wasn't set off balance by new surroundings. *I wish I could talk as easily about my convictions*, Jacie thought.

"Did you ever think about being homeschooled?" Hannah asked, as though now would be a good time to begin.

As they walked, Jacie smiled, waved, and said, "Hi," to many of the students—whether she knew them or not.

"It was never an option at my house," Jacie said.

"Oh, but that's not true! Every family can homeschool! Especially for the elementary and middle school grades. There's so much help out there with homeschool groups. Really, there's absolutely no reason why a child can't be homeschooled these days."

Hannah was so happily convinced that Jacie really hated to burst her bubble. "My mom is a single mom. She's always had to work."

"Oh," Hannah said quietly, as if she hadn't considered that situation.

"But it sounds really positive," Jacie said. "Tell me more."

Hannah opened up again, chatting about her schooling, which Jacie had to admit, did sound a whole lot more fun than her own education had been—so many field trips, family outings, real experiences with foreign languages. Not quite so dull as her own—it made Jacie wish she'd had the opportunity. It also revived the longing she always tried so hard to forget—to be a member of a real, whole, complete family.

"This area is called the Quad," Jacie said, interrupting Hannah. "We call it the Quad, even though it's really a triangle. I guess no one is really sure what you'd call it otherwise—a Tri? So it was easier to keep it the Quad."

"It's very popular," Hannah said, turning every way to look at the groups of students sitting on or at picnic tables, sitting on cement planters surrounding trees, flopped on the grass—generally just hanging out.

One group immediately caught Jacie's attention. "There they are!" She waved her arms over her head. "Alyeria!" she shouted.

A trio of people at a lunch table looked up and waved back.

Hannah looked puzzled. "Which one is Alyeria?"

"It's a place," Jacie explained. "Shouting Alyeria is how we can easily get each other's attention. Those are my best friends. We're also kind of connected by *Brio*—"

"*Brio?*" Hannah asked.

"Yeah. There's this magazine—"

"I know what that is. I get that magazine! I love it!" Hannah's eyes narrowed, her voice dropping from enthusiasm to suspicion. "You mean you're—"

"JACIE!" Becca waved her hand wildly in the air.

"You're a *Christian?*" Hannah asked, sounding shocked.

"Yes," Jacie said, walking quickly toward her friends, hoping to distract Hannah. "Come on! I'll introduce you."

"Hey, everybody. This is Hannah. She's a *Brio* sis and new to school."

"Hi, Hannah," the trio said in unison.

Becca stood up, uncurled her fingers from around a steaming cup of hot chocolate, and leaned across the table, offering her hand. "I'm Becca," she said.

"You never give me a chance to introduce you," Jacie teased.

"That's because you're too slow," Becca retorted.

"Becca is our 'go-for-it' girl. If something needs to be done, she'll do it. She also loves extreme sports," Jacie told Hannah. "If it's a sport and it's dangerous, you can bet Becca is right there in the midst of it."

"What's life if you can't enjoy a thrill once in awhile?" Becca said.

Jacie turned to Solana, who twisted on her seat to face them. "This is Solana. She's the science guru I was telling you about. If you want to know anything about physics, chemistry, astronomy—"

"Or guys," Becca added, receiving a playful backhanded swat from Solana.

"—just ask Solana."

Solana smiled and also shook Hannah's hand. "I feel like I'm meeting some dignitary," she said. "All this shaking-hands stuff."

Hannah laughed. "I'm certainly no dignitary."

"Then let's quit shaking hands."

"And this is Tyler," Jacie said, waving a hand toward the surfer-blond who sat across the table. "He's our token hunk."

Tyler rolled his striking, deep blue eyes. "Don't listen to them. They're always making fun of me. I'm the token *guy* in this group." He stood and leaned across the table to shake Hannah's hand. But Hannah wasn't so eager to reach out her hand this time. She hesitated a moment. When she finally took his hand, she looked into his eyes.

Jacie couldn't help but notice the look that passed between them. She looked away, then said quickly, "You are too our token hunk." She turned to Hannah. "Isn't he gorgeous? The best looking guy at SBHS."

"And all the girls adore him," Solana said. "How could they not? He's got the perfect body."

Tyler's face slowly turned red.

"We adore him, too," Becca added. "Just not in the same way as the other girls. We've known him far too long for that."

Hannah looked awkward. Shy. She dropped her gaze toward the ground. "Um . . . I wouldn't know."

Solana stared at her. "You wouldn't know? Either he's positively hot, or he's not. I think it's one of those things you simply can't *not* have an opinion on. Truth is truth, right, Becca?" Her voice had turned sarcastic.

Becca frowned at Solana. "Back off."

Hannah looked up, confused. "I don't understand—"

"Don't worry," Jacie told her. "They're always butting heads about something. The word 'truth' has a different meaning for Solana than it does for the rest of us."

"They're harmless," Tyler added. "Unless they're talking about you." He flashed Hannah one of his killer smiles.

"Is that for me?" Jacie asked, pointing at the Copperchino cup sitting next to his. She hoped her attempt to distract Tyler wasn't too obvious.

"Oh, I almost forgot," Tyler said. "Here's your hot chocolate. Sorry, Hannah. If I'd known you were going to be here, I'd have gotten you one, too."

Becca and Solana threw Tyler dirty looks which didn't have any affect on his smile at all. He was again oblivious to everything except Hannah.

"I guess what I don't understand," Hannah continued, "is how you can be good friends if you disagree on everything."

"We're good friends," Becca said, "because we've known each other forever."

"Not really forever," Solana corrected. "But ever since the fourth grade. Maybe you could say we tolerate each other." She laughed.

Jacie sat next to Solana. Hannah went around the table and sat next to Becca. "That's not true," Jacie told Hannah. "We *are* best friends and we do more than tolerate each other."

"And what's the connection to *Brio* magazine?" Hannah asked.

"My mom works for the magazine," Tyler said. "And the editor, Susie Shellenberger, likes all the *Brio* readers to think of themselves as family. Sometimes they even think of themselves as sisters and we fall into calling each other that."

"But you're no sister," Solana said, her voice husky. "You're a brother if I ever saw one."

Hannah's aqua blue eyes had grown wide. "Your Mom works for *Brio?* Really? So you know Susie?" She looked at Tyler's face, then quickly down at her hands which rested, folded, on the table.

"Yeah. We all know Susie. She's cool. Funny. My Mom is one of the assistants, so we help out sometimes."

"Editing?" Hannah asked, looking back up and then at the girls.

They all laughed. "Hardly," Solana told her. "Tyler can't spell, Becca wouldn't sit still long enough, and Jacie prefers pictures to words. I'm bored with the articles."

"How can you be bored with them?" Hannah asked. "I like them. They really speak to my heart. They're quite uplifting."

"Uplifting?" Solana asked. "What kind of word is that?" She looked around. "We aren't in church, are we?"

Jacie cringed. She didn't want Solana to go off on Hannah on her first day of school—or ever. She tried to think of something to say, but her mind was blank. Why did it always have to go blank at important moments like this?

"We are in God's presence wherever we are," Hannah said. "Uplifting means they push us toward God."

"Kind of like a push-up bra." Solana laughed at her own dumb joke.

"Solana, quit it," Jacie warned, but couldn't help laughing at Solana.

Hannah looked confused.

"Don't worry," Jacie said. "Not too many people really understand us."

Hannah looked pointedly at Jacie. "I know I don't know you at all, and probably shouldn't say anything. But when it comes to faith, I find I can't keep quiet. How come you didn't tell me you were a Christian?" She sounded almost offended.

"I can't just walk up to people and say, 'Hi, I'm a Christian.'" Jacie felt the familiar pang of guilt. Her answer sounded so lame. Why *couldn't* she let others know who she was and what she believed? Why did her faith seem to be so deep inside her that it was stuck there? The closer she got to God, the more she felt unable to share this private part of herself.

"That's what we're supposed to do," Hannah said.

Jacie could see the *Brio* gang watching the conversation as if it were a game of Ping-Pong. Their heads swiveled back and forth between speakers, their eyes showing great interest in this verbal volley.

"Why?" Jacie asked, wishing instead that she could just say, "Of course you're right. I'll start tomorrow." But she was stalling. Hoping answers that made sense to her would bubble up from some spring of truth inside. But, as usual, all was silent.

"Because we're always supposed to be light and salt. Don't hide your lamp under a bushel. We're all called to be witnesses to everyone at all times."

"Of course," Jacie said, her heart growing heavier with guilt.

"And you have such a great personality!" Hannah said, smiling. Her whole beautiful face brightened with encouragement. Jacie felt captivated by her perfect smile, her wide, innocent, blue eyes. "You are so lucky! You even have perfect dimples. Anyone with your gifts should be the best witness. I mean, you're like sunshine. You wave to everyone. You're nice to everyone. Just in the few minutes we took to walk here, you must have said 'hi' to fifteen people. And some of them were kind of scary looking. You have a great gift, Jacie. It's a shame for you to waste it."

Jacie didn't know what to say. She figured that everything Hannah said was true. For a long time she had wanted to be that kind of person. Becca was that way. Becca spoke of Jesus with such ease. Her words were so genuine that she rarely offended anyone. But Jacie's insides recoiled at the thought of being a perky "Jesus person." She was troubled by the thought of not being what she should be. She just didn't know how she could force herself to do all that.

"Good goin', Hannah," Becca said. "We've been trying to tell Jacie that for a long time."

"Speak for yourself," Solana said. "I don't think Jacie should have to blurt out Bible verses to be a good Christian. I really like the fact that she's not always talking Jesus every time I turn around." Solana threw a teasing grin toward Becca. "Unlike other friends I have."

Becca threw her plastic stirrer at Solana. It was so light it fell in the middle of the table.

"Oh, I'm wounded," Solana said. "Maybe someday you'll learn the laws of energy and motion for lightweight objects."

"You aren't a believer?" Hannah asked Solana.

"No way."

"Why not?"

"I'm not about to give over my intelligence to some narrow-minded religion that preaches intolerance." Solana cocked her head and gave Hannah a fake half-smile.

"Excuse me, Solana. I don't want to be rude to you, but I really must say something to your friends."

Solana shrugged and raised her brows. "Okay. Blurt it out. I'm all for honesty."

Hannah looked at the others. "You aren't doing your job very well if your best friend isn't even a believer. And should you be best friends with her if she isn't?"

Solana nodded at her friends. "She may be a bit on the conservative, Bible-thumping side, but I like her. She's outspoken. She stands up for what she believes."

Jacie felt Solana's words as if they were meant only for her. *Me, the one who can't stand up for anything.*

Tyler ran his fingers through his hair and abruptly changed the direction of the conversation. "Jace. The girls tell me that you aren't going to go to the art conference."

"You're in on this, too?"

"Of course. You're the best, Jacie. We just wish you knew it."

"I wish the new art teacher knew it."

"He, she, or it will soon enough," Solana said.

"He," Jacie said. "And no, he won't. There's not enough room in the class. I don't have art this year."

"How is that possible?" Becca asked.

"What?" Solana shrieked. "That's an outrage."

"It's probably God's will," Hannah quietly said. "I know it's really none of my business, but if you are truly a Christian, Jacie, then you have to know that this must be His will."

"You see?" Solana said. "This is why I don't like God. He supposedly gives a wonderful talent to someone like Jacie, then doesn't want her to use it? That's just plain mean."

"God's ways aren't always our ways," Hannah said gently. "We must accept everything from Him—both the good and the bad."

"Yeah, right," Solana said. She turned her back on Hannah and stared at her hot chocolate.

Jacie knew all those verses. She believed that everything Hannah said was true and from the Bible. But in her heart it didn't feel good. She felt she'd have to accept it, but she didn't want to.

"If you can't go to art class, then that's all the more reason for you to go to the National Art Conference," Becca said.

Suddenly Jacie's heart leapt as if it *felt* the truth rather than just heard it. "But I can't afford it."

"If we're talking about God," Becca said, "it also says in the Bible that nothing is impossible with Him." She looked pointedly at Jacie. "So are you going to go?"

Jacie wanted to go. Oh, how she wanted to go. And now that she couldn't take art, she wanted to go even more. But who was right? Becca or Hannah? Should she just lie back and presume not being able to go was God's will? Or should she trust that God could make it happen?

Hannah looked at Becca as though she were looking at a small child. "The Bible says 'in everything give thanks; for this is God's will for you in Christ Jesus.' Yes, God can do anything. But if He's already done something, we have to believe it's His will, and thank Him for it."

Jacie was confused. More than anything her heart wanted to have art class. To go to the artists' conference. Her heart fairly burst with the wanting of it. It was as though her whole being could not live unless it expressed itself through pictures.

Becca spoke, her voice sounding strained. "Do you think God gave her a gift to ignore?"

"Not all desires are from God," Hannah said.

Becca looked at Jacie. "You *have* to go to the conference. You *have* to fight for a place in the art class."

"We're to be content wherever God puts us," Hannah continued, her voice soft and gentle, caressing Jacie.

"I'll have to think about it," Jacie said to both of them.

"There's no thinking about it as far as I'm concerned," Solana said without turning around. "You belong in both, and I think any God would agree with me."

Jacie jumped up. "Oops! I forgot. I'm supposed to be back at the gym by now. Becca, can you take Hannah to her first class for me?"

Becca glared at Jacie.

"Solana? Can you?"

"Where's she going?"

"L–215." Jacie turned to Hannah. "All classes on the left side of the triangle are L-something. Second floor starts with the number 2, first floor classrooms start with a 1. Classrooms on the right side start with an R—"

"I'm going to L–16," Tyler said. "I'll take her."

Jacie forced a smile. A funny feeling zipped through her stomach.

chapter 4

"Jacie," Mr. Girard said, "I want you to take this gentleman and show him around the school."

"Okay," Jacie said, smiling at Mr. Girard. She turned, and her heart jumped. Leather jacket. Blond, bed-tousled hair. Eyes that bored into her. "Hi," she said. "You drive a motorcycle?"

He nodded, a half smile on his lips. "You drive some sort of pale greenish compact?"

"Yeah." Jacie wondered why she wasn't angry with him. Instead she was captivated by his incredible green eyes. *Solana is going to be so jealous.*

"You two know each other?" Mr. Girard asked.

"Not really," the boy said without taking his eyes off Jacie. "It's just that I nearly ran her off the road by accident this morning."

"*Did* run me off the road," Jacie said.

"Sorry," he said. "I didn't see you. Really, I hope you're okay."

"Where'd it happen?" Mr. Girard asked "In front of the school?" Jacie nodded.

Mr. Girard wagged his head. "We need to do something about that rise in the road."

"I'm Jacie," she said, smiling and sticking out her hand, then feeling like a dork. *Should I shake hands or not? Is that stupid? I never shake hands with kids when I meet them. Why am I doing it now?*

"I'm Damien," he said. He gave her a crooked smile and held out his hand. "Hi, Jacie." He didn't let go of her hand, but stared into her eyes. "Thanks for the tour."

"But I haven't given it to you yet," she said, her voice much smaller and breathier than normal.

"You sure haven't."

"Ahem," Mr. Girard said. "Time for tours."

Damien let go of her hand, but continued to hold her in his gaze. "Sure. Whatever."

Jacie kept smiling. *Okay,* she thought. *How can I get him out of here without running into the* Brio *gang? I don't want him meeting Solana.* And then, it came to her. *Go through the pool area.* She turned to Damien, his eyes once again drawing her. "Do you like to swim?" She felt so lame asking him, but she was trying to drum up some excuse for taking the pool route.

"Sure," he said.

Jacie expected him to explain more, yet she only got the one word from him.

"We'll start with our pool then," she said, pushing on the flat bar to open the door from the gym to the pool. She knew her friends had no reason to go through the pool area.

As Damien moved, everything about him screamed rebel. Bad boy. She could see it in the way he wore his T-shirt. The way he wore his jeans. The way he carried himself.

Jacie was overwhelmed. She couldn't understand her attraction. She wondered if he was a druggie, though. He didn't seem like one. He was too clean, too together, his eyes too bright. He also didn't seem like a violent kid. Probably a quiet rebel. One of those boys who sat in the back of class—never disrupting a teacher or childishly flicking spitwads, but quietly creating a wall around himself so that no one would touch him or speak to him. Teachers rarely spoke to these kinds of kids. But this one was different. And Jacie was trying to give him a tour.

Jacie led him around the school, explaining its history, the students' pride in it, the layout, the teachers, the experimental cafeteria with a mini Taco Bell and Subway and Pizza Hut as meal options. She told him everything she could think of, walking slowly, pointing things out. But every word from her mouth felt stupid. Awkward. As if it was always the wrong thing to say. She, who was usually so easy with words and connecting with people, suddenly could not think of how to phrase the simplest sentence. She smiled a lot and laughed with him as they teased and joked back and forth.

As they walked through the school, jumbled thoughts cluttered her mind. *Who are you? Where are you from? Look at me. Touch me. Let me lean against you. Does he realize I'm a Christian? Would it matter? If it did matter, should I lie about it? JACIE! What are you THINKING? Deny yourself for a GUY?* Where were these thoughts coming from? Why were they so powerful? The intensity of them frightened her.

She was afraid one of the thoughts might suddenly fall through her brain and out of her mouth. She felt a magnetism so strong she wondered if she'd just start leaning against him. It was all she could do to keep a decent distance between them.

She wondered about the things she told him. Were they making sense? Did he know she was stalling? Was she blabbing on and on about nothing? She didn't know. She only knew she was more attracted to Damien than she ever had been to anyone else in her whole life.

"Where are you from?" she finally asked him, realizing that was at least a safe and ordinary question.

"California."

That crooked smile again. She felt like she was melting.

"My dad lives in California," Jacie told him.

"Where?"

"Sausalito. What part of California are you from?"

"East Bay. Antioch."

"Why did you come to Colorado?"

"Forced." Something seemed to flash through his eyes. It was so quick, Jacie almost missed it. If she wasn't so in tune with eyes, she never would have seen it. *What was that? Fear? Pain?*

"I'm sorry."

Damien shrugged. His green eyes became empty.

"I'm glad you're here," she said, then waited until that crooked smile returned, and so did the playful presence in his eyes. She felt swallowed, enveloped in them.

A bell rang.

"I'd better get you to class," Jacie said as the halls filled with students.

"It's right behind you."

"Oh, yeah." She tried to smile. It came out all weird. Her smile stretched her face funny. She was sure of it.

"What's your last name, Jacie?"

"Noland."

"I'll see you later, Jacie Noland."

"Okay."

He disappeared into the room. She felt as if she were under a spell.

Jacie returned to the gym, and discovered the students and teachers were gone. A custodian swept up paper scraps and dirt. Two more custodians folded tables and stowed them in a closet. *That must have been one heckuva tour.*

● ● ●

Jacie stood outside the door of the art classroom. She knew this room better than any other. She'd spent so many hours in there—during class, before school, after school. She had taken advantage of as much time as Mrs. Waisanen would give her.

She began to pace in the hallway, walking back and forth, looking through the window in the door from a distance so her face wouldn't be easily seen. She knew better than to disturb the teacher during the class. This was a touchy matter anyway. No sense in making it worse.

She fidgeted. Her heart started to beat harder as she waited for the passing bell. And wondered what she should say to the teacher.

Hi, my name is Jacie Noland and I would really like to take this class.

Not too bad, but not powerful enough.

I really need this class.

Too whiny.

Every minute seemed to increase her heart rate and nervousness. She scanned the classroom. Every seat was taken, and a couple of students sat on the window sills, their backs to the fall sunshine.

She hoped no one would catch her here. She knew she should be in class. On the first day, and in a position of responsibility with Mr. Girard, Jacie knew she wouldn't get in any big trouble. But she also knew she should be meeting the geometry teacher, not here in the hallway waiting for the bell to ring.

She bit her lip, chewing off a shred of rough, dry skin. She shifted the portfolio under her arm.

The bell rang.

As the students pushed past her, she inched her way into the classroom. The teacher had his back to her. He was erasing "period 4" from the chalkboard and writing "period 5." He had written "Mr. Cornwall" on the other side of the board, and had drawn a decent caricature of himself below his name—small glasses perched on his slender nose, bushy eyebrows, elongated, craggy face.

Jacie waited until he turned around. "Hello, Mr. Cornwall."

He returned her greeting with a weak smile. "Yes," he said.

"I'm not in your class—"

"Are you sure? Everyone else seems to be in my class." He chuckled.

"Everyone but me!" Jacie said. Hoping to butter him up she flashed him her trademark smile and said, "I was looking forward to having you as my teacher. I heard you could probably help me."

He adjusted his glasses and peered over them at her. "How?"

"I'm an artist," she began.

He muffled a chuckle so that it came out a kind of "hmmph."

Feeling deflated, she tried to continue. "And I've hit some rough spots. I was hoping to be in your class, or have some sort of independent study so that I can get beyond this stuck place and become an excellent artist."

Mr. Cornwall dipped his head so far down that his eyes looked like they might disappear into the eyebrows. "Oh my, but that's not possible Miss—"

"Noland," Jacie offered.

"Budget cuts and too few teachers . . . " he shook his head looking sadly at his roll sheets. "There just isn't time or space." He looked up from the sheets at her. "Miss Noland, art is hard. Very hard. You have to be born with talent. You can't just 'become' an artist. You have to be born one."

"But, sir!" she said, feeling tears starting to come up from her eyes. "I believe that—"

"Everyone believes they can be an artist," he said, in a weary voice. "But only a rare handful actually *are* artists. The best thing you can do to avoid certain disappointment is to go home and find something else to do where you'll actually make some money." He turned away from her and began to greet the students who were entering the room.

"Please," Jacie said, starting to untie the ribbons holding her portfolio closed. "Just look at one—"

"I really wish I could help you, Miss Noland. But the truth is that artist or not, there isn't room for you here."

Jacie, raised to always obey authority, picked up her portfolio and left the room.

She felt sick in her whole being. Sick at heart. Sick at knowing there would be no way she could become the artist she wanted to be, the artist she *hoped* she could be. The slam of the classroom door behind her felt like a door slamming inside her heart, closing her off from what she always believed was her future.

● ● ●

Jacie turned off the main highway. Her car bumped over the dirt road as she wound past the modular home of the landowner. When she passed a stand of aspens, she could see a small, windowed shack that looked about ready to fall over. The boards, worn gray with weather and years, barely clung together. It was perfectly lopsided, as if engineered that way. Jacie thought it leaned like an old man against his cane, only in this case the cane was a pine tree.

Her heart warmed. She loved the sight of this shack—her art studio shack only a couple miles from the townhouse she shared with her mom. She supposed no one else knew the shack existed. And if they did know, they didn't know what was inside. The only people who did were her three best friends, her mom, and some guy who really wanted to date her mom, but got turned down. In trying to woo her mother, he had offered the shack on the back part of his property to Jacie. He insulated it for her, and updated the one electrical outlet. Into it Jacie plugged a space heater in winter and a lamp. Even though Jacie's mom refused to date him—or anyone—Russell still let her keep the studio. Because of the wannabe boyfriend's kindness, Jacie had a private place to paint and draw all year round.

Jacie slipped through the door of the little shack. Sunlight poured in from the windows all around. Jacie loved her "art studio." When she drew, if the weather was good, it was mostly outside. She took her pastels, set up an easel, and drew and smudged and considered and thought and drew some more. But she *painted* inside. She didn't know why that was.

She curled up in the overstuffed rocking chair. Equipped with a swivel-rocker underneath, it allowed her to swing from side to side, rock, or stay still. Even though it was covered in hideous brown floral velveteen fabric, Jacie still loved it. She could sit there and go away at the same time. She could slip into the thoughts that plagued her. She could talk out loud to God, and no one else would hear. She could write in her journal or draw in it. She could contemplate her art and wonder why it wasn't going the way she wanted it to.

Some days she wanted so desperately to paint, but nothing seemed to happen. After a few strokes of azure blue, she would put the brush down and pick up another. A cloud of gray. And nothing.

Some days she wanted to paint, but found herself writing in her journal, or staring out the western windows toward the mountain peaks, or thinking about a million things.

Other days she couldn't stop painting. Hours flew by as a person came to life underneath her brushes. She loved those days. She felt energized, alive, fulfilled.

Today she curled up in her chair and took her journal from the table that served as a drawing area and desk.

He's a jerk, she wrote. *A complete jerk. But he's also right, isn't he? There are lots of wannabes in this world, and who's to say my art is any good anyway?*

She thought for a moment, and realized it wasn't fair to call Mr. Cornwall a jerk. He was a teacher who had too many students. Why *should* he consider taking on one more just because she said she was an artist?

The brochure sticking out of the trash can caught her eye. She reached for it and began to read it over again. Part of her was desperate to pursue attending the conference. It seemed like such an answer; it *felt* like an answer. But how could it be an answer when it was so far out of reach? And what if Mr. Cornwall was right? What if she was following some stupid "bunny trail," as her Grandma Noland called them?

God? What do you want from me? she wrote in her journal. *The youth pastor says that other people and your Word help us know which direction to go. So am I supposed to listen to Mr. Cornwall? Was Mrs. Waisanen leaving, and Mr. Cornwall coming so that I would stop trying to be an artist?*

She dropped the brochure into her backpack. It was stupid to keep it, but somehow she didn't want to let go of the dream.

She turned to write more in her journal, but instead began to sketch a pair of eyes. She immediately knew whose eyes she was striving for.

Damien's.

She traded the journal for her sketch pad and drew. She saw them again in her mind. She saw the depth of them. The secrets behind them. The light in them when he smiled at her. But she couldn't seem to transfer them to paper. Page after page of the sketch pad sailed into the air and landed on the floor, discarded petals of a flower—*he loves me, he loves me not. Stop it, Jacie! You don't even know him—he doesn't know you.* But she kept drawing and drawing.

Some days she brought her CD player and worked to music. But today she worked to the music of thunder from the afternoon storm rumbling and echoing in the distant mountains. When her paper ran out, she gathered some sheets from the floor, flipped them over, and tried some more. She tried to draw more than the eyes now, hoping that by sketching more of him she could capture his essence.

She used to do that in the fifth grade. If she could draw the boy she liked, she could refer to the drawing again and again, thinking of him. Smiling. Dreaming. But she could not seem to capture Damien.

"WHY CAN'T I DO THIS?" she shouted in frustration, ripping to shreds her latest attempt. She threw the pieces, then crossed her arms, glaring out the window. A bolt of lightning shot to the ground in the distance. Moments later, thunder rolled by. She grumbled to herself, yelling silently over and over until it came to her. *How can you really capture someone you don't know?*

"I've done it before," she muttered.

chapter 5

Jacie was so intent on her drawing, she didn't hear her friends until they burst through the door, laughing, tumbling over each other like little kids. She would have been briefly angry that they startled her, but they were so funny, all arms and legs and laughter, that she could only smile.

"When are you guys going to grow up?" she asked, starting to laugh.

"NEVER!" declared Solana.

"It's no fun to grow up," added Becca. Then she put her hands on her hips, looking like a coach watching her team lose the game. "Where were you at lunch?"

"You left us stuck with that Hannah girl," Solana said. "She just marched right up to us as though we've been friends our entire lives."

"I told her she could hang with us and be our friend," Jacie said.

"You did what?" Becca asked.

"Without asking?" Solana said.

"Come on," Jacie said, amazed that her friends were being so closed to new people. "We can be nice to a new girl. And what's wrong with having more friends?"

"It's not that, really," Becca defended. "It's just that Hannah's a bit—well, conservative."

"Sheltered," Solana added.

"And that's a reason to not be friends with her?" Jacie asked.

"I'm sorry," Becca said. "I don't know what it is. Maybe it's all the stuff with Alvaro. He's kind of changing our lives drastically. I know it's just temporary—but I guess I just wanted everything to be the same as always here at school."

Solana sighed. "You're always right, Jace. We've got to give the poor girl a chance. We can be her friends until she finds other ones to hang out with."

"And what if she doesn't?" Jacie asked.

"She will," Becca said. "And if she doesn't, I bet she won't really do anything that would change things with us much."

"She *was* pretty quiet when she came up to us at lunch," Solana said. "It was more like she was watching us than anything. Maybe she only speaks up when she's trying to make a point."

Jacie drew her brows together. She thought about Hannah being so afraid and withdrawn before going into the gym for registration. It was true, it seemed the times Hannah spoke and acted confidently was when it had to do with her convictions. "Hannah marched right up to you guys," Jacie said out loud. "*Hannah?*"

"Well, not exactly on her own," Becca admitted. "She came with Tyler. It seems he has appointed himself her personal guardian. He met her at *every* class to make sure she found the next one all right."

"So where were you?" Solana asked, repeating Becca's earlier question.

"I was here in my studio," Jacie said. "I was so discouraged after talking to the art teacher that I got permission from Mr. Girard and Mom to come here. But I have to go to all my classes tomorrow."

"What'd the teacher say?" Becca asked while Solana started looking around the room at all the pieces of paper. She bent down to pick one up.

"He said I should figure out something different to do with my life," Jacie said, feeling discouraged.

"That's *stupid!*" Solana said, waving a piece of paper. "Just look at these eyes. They're perfect."

"No, they're not," Jacie replied. "I can't even draw one set of eyes right."

Solana bent over again to pick up more of the discarded drawings, her long, brown hair falling around her face. "Why are you drawing all these eyes of some guy?"

"I'm not," Jacie protested.

Becca looked at the drawings as Solana handed them to her. "These are definitely a guy's eyes."

"Can't you tell?" Jacie said, hoping the answer she grabbed at didn't sound too phony. "They're Tyler's eyes."

Her friends stared at her. Solana looked at Becca. "Too many paint fumes in this place."

Becca nodded in agreement. She looked at Jacie. "These eyes are all some funky greenish-blue, Jacie. Since when did Tyler have green in his eyes?"

"Maybe he's wearing contacts," Solana said helpfully.

Jacie smiled, latching onto Solana's comment. "I thought I'd see what Tyler looked like with green eyes."

Becca moved around in the little shack, picking up sketches, uncrumpling them. Some had oil pastel color in them. Some were simple charcoal. Some had a black lightning bolt of frustration through the middle of them.

"Who *is* this guy?" Solana asked. "It's obviously not Tyler, or you've really lost every ounce of talent you ever had."

"Don't say that," Becca scolded. "She needs encouragement right now."

"I'm just practicing eyes," Jacie lied, swallowing hard.

Solana put her hands on her hips. "They all look the same. You're going for a specific set of eyes."

"Where did you meet him?" Becca asked, as she looked at each one of the drawings.

"You're both nuts," Jacie said. "You know me. I can draw for hours just trying to get something right." She dropped into the rocking chair.

Solana watched Jacie closely. "What are you hiding from us?"

Jacie's heart thumped in her chest. "Nothing. I wouldn't hide anything from you guys."

"You lie," Solana said. She picked up eyes that stared up at her from the floor. "This is creepy. I swear they're looking right through me. This has got to be someone you know, Jace."

Becca nodded. "Your drawings are always the best when you know your subject real well. Thus!" Becca said, thrusting her finger into the air, "you *must* know these eyes well—and the person attached to them. I bet these are almost a perfect rendition of somebody's eyes."

"No, they're not," Jacie blurted. "I can't capture them right."

Her friends looked at her, then at each other, and smiled.

"I know where she met him," Solana said.

"She's been different ever since she got back from California," Becca added.

Solana nodded. "A Sausalito boy? A tourist?"

"Did your dad meet him?" Becca asked. "Does he even know about it?"

"Would her dad care?" Solana asked. "Or is he too much the typical absent parent who approves of everything just to make sure his kid likes him?"

"Shut up," Jacie said. "You know he's not like that. He might give me guilt-gifts, but he's strict."

"I bet it was when she was painting that landscape of the San Francisco skyline from that curve in the main street in Sausalito," Becca suggested, steering the conversation away from danger. "What's that street?"

"Bridgeway," Jacie said.

"I love that spot."

"That was a good painting," Solana said. "I liked the colors in it." She blew her raspberry gum into a large bubble. When it popped, her brown eyes narrowed as if she were bringing something into focus.

"He was drawn first to the painting—"

"And then he took one look at Jacie's beautiful hair—"

"And he started talking to her—"

"She looked up at him with her beautiful smile—"

"Don't forget her dimples—"

"And laughing eyes—"

"Quit it," Jacie said, laughing. "You're both crazy."

"And then Jacie saw his eyes—" Solana batted her eyes.

"And she was lost in them forever—" Becca said, putting the back of her hand to her forehead. "OH, Joe-y, can I draw your eyes?"

"They're *incredible*," Solana added. "My life will be incomplete if I have to live one more day without drawing those eyes."

The laughter ended abruptly. Jacie felt the heat rise up her neck. "You've really lost it now—"

Solana studied Jacie. "No, we haven't. We're getting it right, aren't we? Come on, Jace—'fess up."

"There's nothing, really." Jacie didn't know how to combat the words that threatened her precarious sense of balance.

"If you can't tell your best friends, who can you tell?" Solana pressed. She moved closer to Jacie. She held up a drawing with green eyes that were almost right, but not quite.

For a split second, Jacie saw him. Her heart jumped. "It's not him," she said, almost breathless.

Solana nodded triumphantly. "So there *is* a him, huh?"

Jacie shook her head, as if the lies would fly off her.

"*Christians* aren't supposed to lie, Jacie," Solana taunted. "Especially *good* Christians like you."

Jacie felt the dagger go right through her. She bent down to pick up discarded drawings and attempted to stuff them into the overflowing trash can. She fought back tears. She fought back the questions she'd had ever since she'd met Damien. *How can I like a boy so much who I just met? How can I fall for a boy I don't even know is a Christian or not? What made me fall so fast?*

Then there were the questions that had gnawed at her for a long time that seemed to be answered in Damien.

And she felt stupid because she didn't even know him.

Becca looked around the floor, picking up and discarding eyes. "I think you really like him, Jacie."

"There's nothing—I mean no one—to like," Jacie said, her mind whirling. She grabbed the clock. "Oh dear. I've got to go start dinner or Mom will be disappointed. Come on."

Becca dropped her stack of drawings to the floor.

Solana stuffed the one that spooked Jacie into her pocket.

Jacie stood in front of her and stuck out her hand. "Give it to me, Solana."

Solana shook her head.

"You can't keep it. You know the rules," Jacie said, her hand still out.

"Your rules are stupid," Solana said.

Becca said, "I don't know why you have a rule that no one else can see your work. You're so good."

"More talented than anyone else at our school, that's for sure," Solana added. "You keep saying that God gives people gifts. Well, if you believe it, maybe you will share it with other people."

"I let you guys see it," Jacie protested.

Becca and Solana exchanged one of their looks. "Big deal," Becca said. "You barely show *us* anything, either. What good is your art if you don't share it?"

"It's not good enough anyway," Jacie reminded her.

"I'm gonna punch you," Solana said. "Anything to knock some sense into you."

"And I'm going to hit *you* if you don't give me that drawing."

Solana laughed. "I'd like to see you try."

"Come on," Becca said. "Jacie's got to get home."

Solana stuck her hand in her pocket. She removed it slowly. The second the drawing appeared, Jacie yanked it from her hands and threw it on the floor.

Becca stared at the eyes on the floor. "You are so amazing, Jacie."

The girls filed out the door. At the last second, Jacie grabbed her journal and the backpack with the brochure stuffed inside.

As Jacie locked the door, Becca suddenly shrieked. "I almost for-got! Duh!" She reached into her pocket and took out a flyer. "Put this with the other one," she said. "If you look at it right, the two can go together."

Jacie took the bright yellow flyer from her. SECOND ANNUAL COPPER RIDGE ART SHOW, the headline read. "I already knew about this," Jacie said. She held the flyer out so they could see it. "Whoever did this isn't an artist. Look at how plain and boring it is."

"Who cares?" Becca said. "Why haven't you already entered?"

"I don't enter these things. I wouldn't win anyway."

"Look how much prize money they're offering."

Jacie let out a huge sigh. "Five thousand dollars. That's a lot of money," she admitted.

"Enough to pay your way to the conference."

Solana opened the car door and flipped the seat forward. She pointed at Becca, then at the back seat. Becca obediently moved into it. Solana replaced the seat then said to Jacie over the top of the car, "Yeah, but you'll never win it—"

"Because I'm not good enough," Jacie agreed.

"No," Solana said. "Because—like you said—you'll never enter. I told you your 'rules' were stupid."

Jacie gripped the steering wheel. *You have to be born with talent . . . Everyone believes they can be an artist . . .* "Can you guys be totally hon-est with me?"

"Yeah," both girls said.

"Am I just a wannabe?"

Solana threw up her hands as though that was the stupidest thing she'd ever heard and stared out her window.

Becca leaned forward. "Jacie, you are so talented. Remember the pictures you drew in fifth grade for the new teacher and he thought you'd traced them off something?"

Jacie smiled. "That was pretty funny."

"Not at the time. We huddled in Alyeria all lunch not playing our pretend games at all, just talking about how we could convince the teacher to let you draw something in his presence."

"*I* was the one who convinced him," Solana said proudly.

"Doesn't your dad tell you how good you are?" Becca asked.

"Dad works with world-famous artists every day of his life," Jacie said. "He mumbles stuff about my work, but mostly he criticizes it."

"Has he ever told you to forget it?" Solana asked.

"No."

"When you visit him, he takes you to all these classes and museums and introduces you to all sorts of famous artists, doesn't he?" Becca asked.

"Yeah," Jacie said. "But he doesn't tell them I'm an artist. They're all too frantic about their own work to care anyway."

"What does your mom say?" Solana asked.

"You know what she says. But she's my *mom*. She's supposed to think everything I do is amazing."

Only music from the radio filled the car for a few moments. Then Becca leaned forward again. "What has Tyler's mom told you?"

Jacie sighed. "That she would like me to do some art for *Brio* magazine."

"Would she do that if your art was awful?"

"I guess not."

Becca said, "She's not going to put her job on the line just because you're her son's friend."

Things were shifting inside Jacie. As trees turned into blurs, she saw her attempts to draw Damien's eyes littering the floor of her studio. She wanted the instruction to know how to do it right. How to capture someone like Damien on paper. How to paint not just the structure of his eyes, but what was *behind* them as well. "I should go for the National Art Conference, shouldn't I?" she asked softly.

"Heck, yeah," Solana said.

"Yes," Becca said more gently. "You should."

"I really, really want to," Jacie said. She paused, thinking about it all. "But an art show?" Jacie asked, shuddering. "What if my work is so bad that people just laugh at it? I couldn't bear it."

"No one will laugh," Solana said, sounding disgusted. "You're too good."

"Money," Becca said. "You're only doing it for the money so you can go to the conference."

Jacie slowed to a halt at the stop sign. The car jerked forward. Solana moaned.

"I'll do it," Jacie said. "Somehow, some way, I'll do it."

"Good," Solana said. "Glad we got that taken care of. Now tell us about this guy."

Becca leaned forward, trying to stare at Solana around the headrest. "Can't you ever think of anything but guys?"

"Sure," Solana said, "but not right now. This is important. Our friend here is hiding something and it has to do with a guy, so I'm determined to find out what it's all about."

While her friends argued, Jacie tried to think quickly. Should she tell them about Damien? Of course she couldn't tell them about him. Becca would give her a lecture, Solana would press for all the details—upset that Jacie got to meet him before she did since she would say she'd claimed "dibs" on him—and frankly, Jacie wasn't ready for either approach. She wanted to keep Damien all to herself.

"What's his name?" Solana asked.

"Don't let her bother you," Becca said to Jacie. "I know there's not really anybody—unless of course you really *did* meet someone when you were visiting your dad last month, but then that really wouldn't mean anything to you anyway, because you would know it was only a three-week relationship which really isn't a relationship at all, it's just something that happens sometimes—a whirlwind romance kind of thing that's just fun for how long it lasts—"

"Goodness, girl, come up for air," Solana interrupted.

"It's just that I certainly hope there's no guy," Becca said, finally sounding really serious. "She made a promise."

Solana scoffed. "You guys made a rash promise to wait until you got married to have sex. That doesn't mean she can't *date*. It also doesn't mean she can't find a cute guy and draw his eyes."

Becca leaned forward between the seats to look at Jacie. "So what I really want to know is, did you kiss him? Because I hope you know better than that. You also made another commitment to not let guys come between you and God this summer, and that means you wouldn't be kissing anyone. So did you?"

"The summer's over," Solana protested. "Let her kiss someone now."

Jacie tried to laugh. She wondered if *thinking* about kissing a boy was the same as doing it. "Don't you think I'd tell you if there was someone? When was the last time I actually had a date? A date would be such huge news, I wouldn't be able to keep my mouth shut."

"True," Becca said.

"I didn't meet anyone in California." *That much, at least, is true.* "I'll give you my dad's e-mail address. He'll tell you the truth." She figured keeping the conversation confined to her visit was the safest way to go. At least she could be totally honest about that.

Solana pouted. "If there's nobody, then there's nobody."

Right. Nobody. But not for long, Jacie hoped.

chapter 6

"It's going to be incredible," Hannah was saying as she leaned against the picnic table Jacie and her friends sat around. Her cheeks glowed pale red as if she'd already gone for a two-mile run that morning before school. She looked exceptionally beautiful. "Of course you guys already know about it. But I didn't find out until my magazine came. I don't know anyone in town, really, yet, so I'd love it if one of you could come to the *Brio* Faith Fest with me." She looked pointedly at Jacie. "I think the information is going to be so helpful."

Solana held up her hands. "There's no way you're getting me to go to some brainwashing marathon," she said.

"No one would expect you to go," Tyler told her.

"Miss Hannah obviously thinks I should," Solana said.

Hannah smiled sweetly. "Of course I would hope that you would eventually know my Jesus. But this event is really for kids who want to learn how to share their faith. That's the most important thing we can do with our lives."

"So now I'm not good enough," Solana said.

Becca made a disgusted noise. "Don't give us that, Solana. You know that's not true. Quit trying to stir up stuff." She looked at Hannah. "Of course you're right."

"Okay," Solana said, picking up her small backpack. "This is my cue to go say hello to the guys at the varsity football table."

Everyone waved good-bye.

"Now we can talk freely about the importance of sharing our faith," Hannah said brightly.

Jacie smiled, pretending to agree with her. She knew she should live that way—standing up in class like Becca did, being able to explain her beliefs without backing down when a teacher or student disagreed. Instead, she became tongue-tied and instantly her mind went blank.

"It's one of my favorite things to go on the beach in Michigan with my family and witness to the people there," Hannah told them. "It's wonderful to hear their stories and talk with them about salvation."

Jacie's stomach flipped. She'd tried doing something like that before with her youth group. All they were supposed to do was ask simple questions from a survey. She was terrified. Some people laughed at her. Most waved her off. Those she did talk to tried to be patient with her when she couldn't seem to speak sentences that made any sense. She was so humiliated. "I can't do that," she said.

"Oh, sure, you can! Every Christian can do it—*should* do it," Hannah said. "This conference would be perfect to get you comfortable with witnessing. They'll teach you what to say and how to say it. It really isn't hard."

Tyler moved his fingers through his hair, pushing it out of his eyes. "I was already planning to go." He leaned forward and smiled at Hannah.

Jacie and Becca exchanged glances. *Yeah, he'd like to go all right. But not to learn how to witness.*

"How about you, Becca?" Hannah asked, oblivious to the meaning behind Tyler's words and looks.

Becca shrugged. "Sure. I'm always up for a giant rally. I love being around lots of Christians my age who believe the same things I do."

Jacie sighed. Maybe she needed this *Brio* convention. She'd been feeling so inadequate lately. She couldn't seem to share her faith at all. And God *must* be disappointed with her.

"I'll go," she said in a small voice. *Maybe if God is happy with my witnessing, He'll help me get to the art conference somehow.*

She stopped her thoughts. Why would God help her to go to the National Art Conference where she wasn't learning something spiritual? She knew the scholarships for the *Brio* rally Hannah had told them about would come through for her. God *wanted* her to share her faith. She knew that. Going to the National Art Conference surely was not on His list of important things for her to do. How would going to a secular art conference make her a better Christian?

Jacie moved through the day preoccupied. She could hardly keep her mind on her classes. It was a good thing that she automatically doodled while she half-paid attention to the teachers. At the end of the class period she thought she hadn't heard a thing. But when she looked at the drawings all over her pages, she noticed little pictures of things the teacher had been talking about. In English Lit, she'd drawn little pictures of a crabby woman with her hair in a bun and two characters beneath her—one with her chin up in the air, looking haughty and full of herself. The other was turning away from someone who was black. Below that, she'd drawn a funny-looking roundish sort of man, two cities on opposite sides of the page, with a dog chasing its tail. She presumed they were going to read *Pride and Prejudice* and *A Tale of Two Cities* that semester.

Every class was like that. During lunch, her friends teased her that she was drawing incessantly to find the perfect piece to submit to the art contest. Jacie hardly heard them, her hands drawing, her mind trying to figure out how in the world she could come up with so much money for the conference. She thought about asking her dad. He might help her. He might not. She was afraid to ask him. Afraid he'd tell her she wasn't good enough. Besides that, she knew he didn't have enough money to pay for the whole thing. No, it was too much to ask for.

After lunch, she blindly walked through the halls to her next class. "Jace."

Jacie turned to smile at Tyler. "You lost your Greek goddess," she told him. "What did you do with her?"

Tyler blushed. "She knows how to get to her classes alone now."

He fell into stride beside her. Once Tyler was alone with her, it happened. It always did. Jacie walked differently. She felt more confident. More full of life. Happier. Funnier. Just being with Tyler made her feel as though she was okay. She felt *comfortable* with him. She told her mom that once. "It's like I'm cuddled under Grandma's quilt in the middle of Mt. Cutler trail—you know the part where you can see the mountains, the waterfall, *and* the prairie all in one view?"

Her mother nodded. "Where you and I had a peanut butter and jelly picnic once."

"I feel like there's nowhere else I can be myself. I feel like that with Tyler. Completely accepted. Like he's the brother who will watch out for me and care for me."

Her mom had kissed her on top of her head as she whisked by, dust rag in hand, on her way to her bedroom. "Everyone needs someone to watch out for them."

Jacie jumped up and followed her mom. "Who is there to watch out for you, Mom?"

Her mother had shook her head. She picked up each piece of an antique dresser set, dusting each one and laying them on the bed.

Jacie stood between her mother and the dresser. "Who, Mom?"

"It's not time for me yet," her mother had answered so softly Jacie almost hadn't heard.

Now Tyler took hold of Jacie's elbow. "Stop."

Jacie turned to look at him. Kids swarmed around them like a creek bypassing the stones in the middle of it. Tyler looked awfully serious. His blue eyes didn't dance with laughter. He didn't move the strands of hair that dangled into his face. "I've been thinking."

Normally Jacie would have said something to tease him. *Thinking? Why Tyler, that would be a first.* But she knew better than to tease Tyler when he was serious. So she just looked at him, waiting.

"I really want you to go to that art conference."

"Me, too."

"Here," he said, stuffing something into her hand. "It's not much, but I think it could at least give you a start."

Jacie opened her hand. "Ten dollars?" Instantly she thought of two things. *Ten dollars won't go very far at all. It's not even a drop in the bucket.* She mentally kicked herself for the bad attitude and spoke her second thought: "Tyler, that's so nice. Why would you do this?"

Tyler looked at the floor. "It's not much." Then he looked at her. He took her hands in his. She almost caught her breath. He looked directly into her eyes. "I believe in you, Jacie. I believe this is something you need to do. I wish it was a lot more. But I figured a little bit would at least let you know how much I think you should go, and encourage you to not give up."

Tyler let go of her hands and took off down the hall. "I don't want to be late!" he called to her.

She smiled. It was so like Tyler. He couldn't be serious for very long. Serious made him uncomfortable.

Jacie clenched the ten-dollar bill and kept it in her hand the rest of the day. *Someone believed in her.* Now if she could only believe in herself.

● ● ●

At work, the hours flew by. Girls still shopping for their back-to-school clothes swarmed through Raggs by Razz, taking armfuls of the latest fashions to the dressing rooms. Jacie tried to keep up with getting them into rooms, out again, keeping track of who had how many items, and retrieving the discarded clothing.

Afterward, Jacie felt worn out. She called her mom and received permission to stop by Copperchino before going home. It was only two doors down from Raggs, so she often went there to de-stress after work. She chose a small table in the dark back corner of the coffee shop—the table nearest the bookshelves filled with old novels. She removed *A Tale of Two Cities* from the shelf and opened it. The pages smelled old and perfect. She lifted the opened book to her nose and inhaled. It wasn't quite the same as the fragrance of her paints, but it had a sense of adventure all its own. Writers told stories with simple word pictures, putting them together, and if they were skilled and fortunate, a great story emerged on the other side.

She slowly took in another breath. *I want to paint stories. I want my work to tell a story just as these books do. One scene. One moment in time. Truth.*

Her favorite English teacher had told her that fiction captures truth in a way nonfiction never can—a deeper truth; the heart of it.

That's what I want to do, she breathed.

"What?" a voice said, startling her.

Jacie dropped the book, lifted her head, and opened her eyes. Her cheeks flamed with heat, and even more so when she saw the green eyes. "Hi," she said softly, feeling incredibly foolish.

"Do you mind?" he asked, his head tilted to one side, his green eyes looking directly into hers. His right hand was gesturing at the curve-backed chair across the table from her.

She couldn't speak, so she merely shook her head. Actually, she didn't know if she minded or not. Under other circumstances, she'd love to have him there. But since he caught her sniffing a book and talking to herself . . .

The chair scraped the floor as he sat down. "I won't bother you," he said, nodding at her book.

"It's okay," she said. "I was just looking at a book we have to read for English."

He seemed to be restraining a smile. "*Looking* at?" he asked.

Jacie sighed, then laughed at herself. "Okay, I confess. You caught me *sniffing* a book."

His smile broke free from the restraints. "A girl after my own heart." He reached over and took the book from her. He opened it, closed his eyes, and inhaled heartily. A satisfied smile crossed his face, and he opened his eyes. "One of the best." His glance fell to the car-ryall bag on the floor next to her. "*Neo-Impressionist Art?*" he said, reading the title. "So you must be an artist."

"Yes. How'd you know? Lots of people read art books."

He held up his hand, rubbing his thumb and his first two fingers. "Your fingers."

She looked down and blushed, ashamed of the colors clinging to her left hand. Charcoal. Pastel. She tucked her hand into her lap.

"No!" he said. "I think it's great. It's good to have something you're passionate about."

"What's *your* passion?" she asked, then was immediately sorry she'd questioned him. A look of pain passed through his eyes and was gone.

He shrugged flippantly in response. "Nothing."

"Maybe you haven't found something to be passionate about yet."

"It's no big deal. Maybe I'll get passionate about the mountains. Everyone else around here seems to be."

Jacie could tell it *was* a big deal. And that he *did* have passion. But she could see it was something too painful to push.

"You're right about that," she said. "We're mountain-lovers through and through. I do have a soft spot in my heart for the San Francisco Bay. I miss the mountains when I'm in Sausalito with my Dad, and I miss the Bay for the first few weeks I'm back in Colorado."

A small grin crept over his lips. "The Bay." He nodded. "Nothing like the Bay on a warm spring night. No fog. City lights kind of wiggly on the water."

Jacie closed her eyes and could see it. Smell it. She could hear the jazz from so many coffeehouses. Visualize some of the quaint street corners.

"So you like jazz as well as art, I see."

Jacie's eyes popped open. *Can he read my thoughts?* Then she realized she'd been moving to the jazz music over the speaker. She blushed for the second time.

"It's okay," Damien told her. "You can bounce to the music if you like."

"I don't even realize I'm doing it," Jacie told him. "It just gets into my skin and I can't seem to *not* move to certain music. Do you like jazz?"

"I like all kinds of music."

"Who's your favorite jazz artist?"

"Miles Davis's *Kind of Blue* is my all-time favorite CD. Scotty Wright is my favorite soloist."

"Who's that? I've never heard of him."

"He had quite a following in Northern California. Not many people know him. But those who've heard him, love him." His gaze zeroed in on her. "I'll have to let you hear some of his music sometime."

"I'd like that," Jacie said, trying not to sound too eager. What she wanted to do was say an emphatic, "YES! Can I come over to your house tomorrow?" but knew that would be a bit much for anyone—including herself.

● ● ●

Jacie floated home on a cloud of something that made her feel complete inside. Her mom tried to talk to her after she walked through the door, but Jacie felt disconnected from everything around her. Nothing seemed real. Nothing seemed quite the same.

She wished she could talk to her mom about it. But she knew how it would end. Her mother, instead of understanding her feelings for Damien, would be worried about Jacie liking a guy Mom hadn't met. And frankly, Jacie didn't want to hear it now. Instead she wanted to close her eyes and relive every moment—including the one where he gently touched her arm as she left. "I'll see you in school," he had said. Jacie could only nod. He'd climbed aboard his bike and zoomed away without looking back. But he'd raised his hand in the air. Jacie had raised hers in response, frozen to her spot on the sidewalk.

chapter

Within five minutes of him leaving, I missed him. No. I missed him right away. Is that crazy or what? How can I miss someone I just met? I used to be glad that we had the biggest school in Copper Ridge. Now I wish it was smaller—it would increase the chances of just running into him by "accident."

I wonder when I'll see him again.

I've got to stop thinking about him.

"Where's Tyler?" Solana asked the next day after school as the girls sat at "their" table.

"Hannah's taking pictures of him with his guitar," Becca said, rolling her eyes.

"Uh-oh," Solana said. "I hope he doesn't play for her."

Jacie smiled. "Of course he will."

Becca seemed lost in her own world. She had that stare as though she looked through the tree in line with her gaze. "I hope she makes new friends soon."

"I thought we were talking about Tyler," Solana said. She flipped up the ends of her long hair, peering at them for split ends.

"It's probably hard for her," Jacie told Becca. Sometimes she wished Hannah had more new friends, too. But she wouldn't wish loneliness on anyone. And a girl like Hannah already had a few strikes against her.

"No harder than it is for anyone else," Becca said. "She just doesn't seem to be trying." Her crossed leg began to bounce up and down, her foot wagging up and down, giving her leg more nervous energy.

"Shhh," Solana said, jerking her chin upward as if pointing behind Becca.

Becca and Jacie turned to see Hannah and Tyler approaching. Hannah stopped a few feet away and began snapping pictures with her manual Nikon 35mm camera.

"Stop!" Becca said, shielding her face. "I don't want you to take my picture. My nose always looks gigantic in pictures."

"Jacie," Tyler said, his voice bright. "Hannah's an artist, too! Isn't that cool?" He sat on the top of the picnic table.

"Really?" Jacie asked. "What's your medium?"

Hannah looked confused. "Photography," she said hesitantly. "Black-and-white is what I really like. The contrasts can bring out the sharpness in things." She looked at Tyler as if for help.

Becca snorted. Solana's eyebrows shot up.

"Oh," Jacie said, her voice falling. She should have known. She should be used to people claiming to be artists by now. How many times had she heard, "I'm an artist!" only to find out the person liked to color when they were little? Or they doodled when they were bored.

"Jacie's a *real* artist," Becca said. "She paints and draws so well. You know exactly who and what she's painted."

"I'm not really that good," Jacie said.

"Can I see some of your work?" Hannah asked. She tucked a wayward strand of hair back into the bun that held her long hair off her back.

"No, you can't see it," Solana told her. "Her work is private. No one sees it."

"I'm sorry," Jacie said kindly. "It's just that I don't feel comfortable—"

"*We* see it," Tyler said.

"*WE* are close friends," Becca said pointedly.

Tyler's blond brows pulled together. "Hannah's a new friend," he said.

Solana looked at him and rolled her eyes. "But *Hannah* was not a part of Alyeria," she said.

"Then let's take her there!" Tyler said brightly.

Jacie and the others glared at him so hard, he put up his hands. "Okay, okay," he said. "I just thought—"

"Well, you thought wrong," Becca said.

"Alyeria?" Hannah said, as if oblivious to the tension in the air.

"Alyeria is our secret place," Jacie told her. "Remember I called that name out the first day?"

"Oh, yes, I forgot. Do you mind if I ask where it is?"

"It's in a grove of aspens on our elementary school playground," Becca told her. "Not really special to anyone else. It was just what we built there."

"We were all in the same fourth-grade class—"

"With Mr. Dacus—"

"Ugh! He was *such* a boring teacher."

"But a good athlete," Becca reminded them.

"Anyway, we girls all loved to imagine more than we liked playing on the school yard."

"Except for me," Becca added. "I liked the sports. But I got tired of smacking a rubber ball against a wall and the other things kids did at recess. I was fascinated by Solana's and Jacie's imaginations and soon joined in."

"We'd hide and imagine we were all sorts of things and people," Jacie said wistfully. "Mostly stuff with castles—fairy tales."

"What about Tyler?" Hannah asked.

"Well, one day he came snooping around."

"I saw them crawling through some bushes into the stand of trees," Tyler said. "I waited a few minutes and snuck in after them."

"We didn't hear him—we were so into our story for the day which had to do with unicorns—"

"That was me," Jacie offered.

"And a prince—"

"I could tell they needed a warrior," Tyler said. "A hero. So I just joined in."

"I was ready to kick his—"

"Solana!" Becca interrupted.

"Okay, so I was ready to boot him out of there. But he just picked up a stick and joined right in."

"It was like he knew exactly what to do," Jacie said.

"We've been best friends ever since."

"That sounds like so much fun," Hannah said wistfully.

"It was the best!" Solana said.

Jacie stood outside the classroom, shaking. She didn't want to be there. She reached for the handle, then pulled her hand back as if it were hot to the touch. She stood there, breathing hard, swallowing more than she needed to.

She held her breath.

She reached again and yanked her hand away before she could open the door.

She stared at the knob in the same way Tyler's cat would stare at the door leading to the outside, as if it would open by magic.

If she really *were* desperate to be good, she told herself, she would do this. She wouldn't be afraid.

She took another deep breath and opened the door.

Mr. Cornwall looked up from his desk. "May I help you?"

"I . . . uh . . . I was in here the other day—"

Mr. Cornwall dropped his pen to the desk. "I believe I told you there was no room in my class."

"I understand that, sir," she said, clutching a small folder of charcoal sketches behind her.

"Then why are you here?"

"I wondered if I could be your assistant." Her mouth felt dry and her words came out sounding sticky.

Mr. Cornwall removed his glasses and looked at her. He said nothing.

Jacie had never been good at talking with authority. She felt intimidated. "I thought maybe you'd need the help since you have so many students."

He sighed. "In theory that sounds good. But honestly, I've found that assistants are generally more of a burden than a help, Miss—"

"Noland."

"Miss Noland, I do not wish to be unkind. However, there is nothing much for an assistant to do in an art class. They can take roll and that is about it. Assistants, as a rule, are at a loss in an art class when it comes to helping other students. You see, helping art students is a very individual, subjective work based on years of experience as a teacher."

He looked down at her, his bushy brows pulled together in one thick, gray line.

"May I leave a folder—" she brought it out from behind her back.

"I don't know what difference that would make." He picked up his pen and turned to focus on the work before him.

She stretched out her folder, the offering of her soul now so close to the fire . . .

"I'm sorry. I really and truly don't have time for even one more moment. I'm up late every night evaluating. I simply don't have more to give." Without looking at her, he said, "You are dismissed now, Miss Noland."

No time. Nothing. She turned and walked out of the room. *Why couldn't he at least have taken two more minutes to look at my work?* She

stuck in the sky

leaned against the wall and started to cry. *I know. I know. He's not trying to be mean. He simply doesn't have a spare moment for someone who isn't his student.* She always hated crying, but this time she couldn't help it. The tears burst forth of their own accord, spilling out from the place inside that felt so hopeless. She slid down the wall and sat on the floor, her back against the lockers. *How can I draw, God? How can I get better if I don't have training? It's not like Mr. Cornwall can give me advanced training. But he could at least give me some guidance.*

She felt a presence in front of her. A hand reached out and gently moved her hair away from her face. "Jacie? What's wrong?"

Jacie saw him, shiny and blurred by her tears. She put her head down again, ashamed. She shook her head, feeling stupid that of all the people to catch her in her tears, it would be Damien.

He squatted to get below her chin, then tried to look up into her face. He touched her arm, gently trying to pull her hand away from her face. "It's okay to cry," he said as if reading her thoughts. "Do you want to talk about it?"

She shook her head. "No," she whispered. But she really did want to talk about it. She wanted to pour out all her frustration and desires that were so much a part of her. But she didn't know Damien. She didn't know if he would make fun of her. Or tell her everything would be okay.

"Come on," he said. "Let's go get some coffee." He stood, his hand out to help her up. She took it, letting him give her the balance she needed.

As they walked down the hall, he barely touched the small of her back—like her father did when he was being a gentleman and taking her to a nice place to eat. He'd open the door, then barely touch her as if to guide her forward.

Jacie walked without speaking, and so did he. Together they moved through the hallway and out the back door. Damien threw his leg over a Harley with orange flames streaming back on a black gas tank. He jumped and the motorcycle came to life. He motioned for her to get on.

She sat on the black leather seat, but didn't know what to do with her hands or her folder.

"Tuck your folder inside your sweater," Damien called over the roar of the engine. After she did so, he reached behind and took her right hand and put it around his waist. He motioned for her to do the same with her left. "Lean into me."

Jacie hesitated.

"It's okay. You'll ride better."

She leaned forward, her cheek against the leather of his jacket. He touched her hands clasped at his waist, then took hold of the handle-bars.

Jacie had never ridden a real motorcycle. She'd been on little dirt bikes with Becca and Solana when Becca's family had taken them all camping near a dirt bike trail.

This, however, was entirely different.

At first, Jacie hung on, afraid of their speed. At the same time, she was fully aware of this strange hug she and Damien shared. She could smell his scent for the first time—musky, male, clean. She kept her eyes closed—both to concentrate on his smell and to block out the speed. But then, as they easily angled around a curve, she opened her eyes and watched the trees blur. She began to loosen her death grip. She looked around Damien and watched the world pass by. Familiar sights took on new perspective from the back of a bike. Waves of green and blue sped up and yet became clearer. She noticed things she hadn't noticed before.

Too soon, they were at Copperchino. With lattes in hand, each sitting on opposite ends of a loveseat. Jacie curled, her legs tucked under her. Damien had one leg angled on the sofa, the other on the floor.

Damien looked at her without speaking. His face looked invit-ing—as though it *would* be okay to share with him. Her mind battled, and she breathed deeply. She looked into her cup as if that would tell her whether or not she could be honest with him. She looked at Damien.

"The art class is full," she told him.

"I take it you've tried to talk to the teacher."

Jacie nodded. She started telling him the story, little by little. Each piece she gave him didn't bring on huge reactions like it had with Hannah or Becca or Solana. Just understanding.

"I'm sorry I was crying," she said. "I really hate to cry."

"It sounds like you had every reason to."

"I thought guys hate it when girls cry," Jacie said, wiping the latte foam off her upper lip.

"I don't know about other guys," Damien said. "I only hate it when girls cry in order to manipulate me."

Jacie looked down at her coffee. She knew so many girls who were proud of their ability to do just that.

Damien spoke. "I guess we also get frustrated when we don't know how to help."

"I don't know about other girls," Jacie said, smiling. "But you just did a perfect job of helping."

"Really?" Damien asked, a smile crossing his face. "I'm glad."

For a few minutes they sat there, sipping their coffee. Jacie thought it odd that she was comfortable with the silence. That was unusual. Usually she felt that when two people were together, there should be talking. But now it didn't matter.

As she sat, sometimes gazing at him, sometimes at others in their own conversations, she couldn't help but wonder at the two sides of Damien. At the contradictions in him. On the one hand, he looked like a bad boy. Everything about him screamed it. Yet he wasn't that way if you talked to him. Was the bad boy image only a cover-up, a wall to keep people away?

If so, why had he let her in?

Or had he?

chapter 8

"Movie," Becca said. "My place." She bent over to unlock her bike. Grabbing her clanging dog tags, she stuffed them inside her T-shirt. The friends clustered around her.

"Seven o'clock?" Solana asked.

"Six if you want pizza and Coke. Five if you want to swim."

"What if we want to play basketball?" Tyler asked.

"Bring Nate Visser and you can come anytime," Becca teased.

"I just might do that," Tyler teased back.

Jacie made a face. "I have to work."

"Come after," Tyler said.

Hannah stood in the midst of them, her head swiveling back and forth as she tried to keep up with the rapid-fire conversation.

"I hate starting a movie in the middle," Jacie said. "I can't follow it."

"Come anyway. We're probably watching something we've already seen," Becca said. "I don't have any money to rent one. I used up my movie rental allowance."

"And I'm too stingy," Solana said. "I'm saving money for Homecoming."

"Do you know who you're going with yet?" Jacie asked.

"No. But I'll find somebody." She winked. "Or somebody will find me."

"They always do," Tyler said. He turned to Hannah. "Come to Becca's, okay?"

Becca made a small face at Jacie while Hannah's head was turned toward Tyler. Jacie shrugged. She didn't really mind the idea of Hannah coming. Maybe they'd get to know each other better. But since Jacie didn't know if she was going to be there or not, she kept quiet.

"I don't know if I can," Hannah said. "My parents don't know you."

Tyler grinned. "To know me is to love me."

"I mean, all of you." Hannah made a sweeping motion with her arm.

"You can call Becca's parents," Tyler offered. "They'll give your parents all the reassurance they need."

Becca nodded her head, but reluctantly. Jacie couldn't figure out why. Usually Becca invited everyone within hearing distance to her house. She loved having people over; the more kids, the better the party. And parties were best at Becca's. Her parents were always there—not hovering, but making sure everything was cool. There was always tons of food and soda. Her house was huge and full of fun stuff—Ping-Pong and pool tables, huge television with a great sound system, and the best hi-tech movie player available. Even though there was a pool in their yard, it was still large enough to string up a volleyball net, or to play football or soccer. They even had a half-basketball court.

"I'd need a ride," Hannah said, sounding hopeful.

"I'll pick you up," Tyler told her.

Hannah shook her head, looking at her feet. "I'm not allowed to ride with boys." Her cheeks flushed.

"Tyler's not a boy," Solana said. Hannah's head popped up, confusion on her face. "He's one of us. A tamer, safer boy you will never meet."

"It doesn't matter," Hannah said, shifting her armload of books. Jacie wrinkled her nose. Why didn't Hannah have a backpack like everyone else? Jacie would have to find out, maybe give her an old one if money was a problem.

"My parents feel that being alone with any boy is potentially dangerous," Hannah explained.

"Sure is," Solana said with a wicked smile.

"Even a Tyler-boy?" Becca asked, swinging her leg over the sissy bar of the bike. She straddled the frame and adjusted her backpack.

"*Any* boy," Hannah said.

"What about going on a date?" Solana asked.

"I'll be courting," Hannah told them, smiling. "I'll only spend time with a boy when he's probably the one I'll marry. And then only in the presence of my parents."

"And you're *smiling?*" Solana asked, horrified. "I sure hope you're joking."

Tyler's face fell. He moved his hand through his hair as if that would clear his mind of whatever suddenly flashed through it.

"I think it's wonderful," Hannah told the stunned group. "Think of how much pain I'll avoid."

Jacie felt a stab of something. Maybe she was supposed to agree with Hannah, but in her heart she didn't want to. Right now she'd accept a little pain in exchange for one more touch from Damien.

"Solana can pick you up then," Tyler offered.

Solana put her hands on her hips. "Yeah, right, Tyler. I was going to go with you."

Hannah brightened. "Well, if there will be a girl in the car, that should be okay."

"Done!" Tyler said, poking his index finger into the air.

After giving Hannah her phone number, Becca took off with a wave. Hannah ran toward an older model white passenger van. The woman inside looked like an older version of Hannah, with shorter hair. Tyler exited toward his Escort clunker while Solana and Jacie made their way to Jacie's Tercel.

● ● ●

Jacie had one hour before she needed to be at work. She curled up in her chair. Instead of her sketch pad, she took up her journal and pen. She bit her bottom lip and started to write the confusion that bubbled up inside her.

Hannah isn't going to date. That is so weird to me. I can't imagine not spending time with different guys in order to figure out what I really want in personality and other stuff. But, since Hannah's life is so close to God—I mean her whole life, including school, has been about God—then maybe she knows more than I do. So maybe courting is the best. Does God talk about it in the Bible?

Being around Hannah makes me think more about my faith. I go to youth group on Wednesday nights and to church on Sundays. We talk about faith a lot. But for Hannah it seems to be more rigid. Is that what faith is about? It is for her.

Faith. What does it mean to me? I wish I knew. I listen to Hannah and I feel so inadequate. I watch Becca stand in front of class like it's no big deal, sharing her beliefs in a respectful and honest way. But my brain doesn't seem to work. It goes completely blank. Everything I've ever known and believed is suddenly gone.

> Why can't I be like them? Why does it seem that the closer I get to God, the more I seem to bury my faith deeper inside me? It's like I'm scared that if I share it, then people are going to tear up something that's precious to me. It would be like taking my best drawing to the art show and having everyone point at it and laugh. I couldn't stand it.
>
> Oh God. Can You really forgive me for not being a better Christian like Hannah and Becca? Can You forgive me for having this ache inside to paint? To draw? I want to ask You to provide the money for the National Art Conference, but I'm thinking that wouldn't be right to ask. But I can't not ask.

She began to draw a flower in the corner of the journal, its petals falling like tears into a pile at the bottom of the page. She began to pray again onto the paper.

> I am most afraid of two things. First, I'm afraid to talk to You about Damien. I'm afraid You will tell me I can't see him again. But he fills up some empty place inside that no one else ever has. I feel like that hole is gone when he's around. So I don't want You to say no to him. And I'm afraid to talk to You about my art because You might take that away, too.

● ● ●

After work, Jacie walked to her car parked around the corner. A piece of paper lay against the windshield, tucked under the wiper.

> *Meet me at the Falls tomorrow for a lunch hike—*
> *if you can. 11:00.*
> *Damien*

She folded the paper and stuck it in her pocket. She thought briefly about going to Becca's. She looked at her watch—9:40. She decided she would rather go home and draw before going to bed.

The next morning at precisely 11:03, Jacie opened the door to her car and put one foot on the dirt. She stopped and pretended to be searching for something in her glove box. *You can do this.* She took a deep breath. *But what if I do something stupid? What if he doesn't like me?* She slathered her lips with Chapstick and dropped it back into the ashtray. She closed it and stepped out of her car, dragging her backpack with her.

Damien leaned against his bike, chewing on a piece of straw, watching her. "Ready?" was all he said.

She nodded, feeling stupid.

Silently she followed him up the trail. The day was perfect. Warm, but not hot. Clouds dappling the sky, but not threatening lightning. The falls roared to the right of them. A hiss of spray hung in the air. In moments, they would wind away from the falls and through the trees would be a spectacular view. She wanted to say something, but nothing came to mind. Well, nothing that wouldn't sound completely idiotic, that is.

When they rounded the curve, the view once again stopped her cold. She couldn't move another inch without trying to pull it inside herself.

To her right, the mountains stretched up to over 14,000 feet at the tallest peak, an old man's face—craggy and jagged—worn rough with age and weather. To the left the mountain dropped to the prairie. It lay flat and brown with houses and trees sprouting from it.

Trees of all kinds climbed the slopes until they reached the timberline. She could tell where stands of aspens mingled with the pines, for they spattered the green with a bright gold as they signaled fall's short stay. Rock formations broke the masses of green and gold, looking as though they had dropped from the sky and landed in the center of the trees, their wonderfully odd shapes formed by years of snow and ice. Most looked like a child's early attempts at using clay to make animals or other creations. When she was little, Jacie often thought these rocks must have been Jesus' early attempts at forming things. And God, the proud Father, put them on display anyway. She smiled to herself. *I would never tell anyone this, but I still like to think they're God's clay creations.*

Early morning or evening was Jacie's favorite time to come up here with a sketch pad. At those hours every crevice in the rocks was highlighted by the sun's low rays.

She closed her eyes and drank in the air—crisp and cold, smelling blue. Even with her eyes closed she could see the beauty in front of her as if her eyes were open. Yet, with her eyes closed, she could somehow "see" more clearly.

When she opened her eyes, Damien was standing quietly, his gaze turned toward the view. He seemed to sense she was ready to move on and turned to her. He smiled and began moving up the trail again.

Jacie couldn't stop the words from coming out. Hiking did it to her every time. It made her sense God's presence like nothing else. "Damien."

He turned to walk backwards. "Hmmm?"

She pointed, but not soon enough. He stumbled against a rock. His arms flailed and she caught his arm, but he fell anyway. They both laughed.

"Girls will do anything for an excuse to touch a guy," he teased as he dusted off his shorts.

"ME!" she shrieked. "YOU were the one who *pretended* to fall."

"Oh, yeah," Damien said. "As if some *wimpy* girl could help someone as strong and masculine as me."

"AUGH!" Jacie exclaimed. "You wish."

"Truth hurts," Damien said, spinning around and beginning to walk up the trail.

Jacie picked up a small pebble and heaved it at his hairy legs. She missed.

Without turning around, Damien said, "Girls are such bad shots."

"And boys have such ugly legs."

Damien burst into laughter. "Yeah, we do, don't we? Oh well, it doesn't bother us too much. We accept it much better than girls accept fat thighs."

"Are you saying I have fat thighs?" Jacie asked, horrified.

Damien swung around and grabbed both her shoulders in his hands. He looked her straight in the eyes. She could tell he was dead serious. "No, you don't have fat thighs. You don't have fat anything. And I will never tease about anything that's true."

He let go and turned back to his hiking. "What were you going to say?"

"Huh?"

"Right before I fell. You were going to say something."

Immediately her heart jumped in her chest and started beating triple its normal speed. She licked her lips, deciding she needed water already. She reached into her hiking pack and took out her water. She took a swig. "I was going to ask if you ever thought about God."

"Not anymore."

"Why?"

"I just don't, okay?"

"Did you used to think about Him?"

"Yes."

"Then how is it possible that you don't any more?"

"Easy. I don't talk about Him. I don't think about Him. He ignores me. I ignore Him." Damien's voice had grown hard.

"Do you want to come to church with me?"

"I told you. I don't do God."

"Why not?"

"God doesn't care about me, so I don't care about Him."

"Yes, He does."

"You don't know, Jacie."

"God cares about everyone."

A disgusted snort came from Damien. He shook his head. "Jacie. Don't be stupid. I didn't think you were like that."

"Did you ever go to church?"

Damien stopped and turned around. "I don't want to talk about this. Accept me as I am or don't be my friend." He moved ahead on the trail.

See, God?! Jacie screamed inside. *This is why I don't like talking to people about You. They just get mad and don't want to hear it anyway. Talking about You seems to ruin friendships.*

"I'm sorry, Damien."

Damien turned and stopped. He looked directly into her eyes. "I'm not mad at you, okay? It's not your problem. It's mine. Just don't talk about God and we'll be okay."

"Okay," Jacie said. But her thoughts churned. *But God is such a part of my life! He confuses me, but I'm still trying to figure Him out and how life works as a Christian. If we can't talk about God, then our friendship can't be as deep as it could.*

The realization stopped Jacie dead. *But if I stay with Damien, then maybe I can bring him back to God. Maybe that's why we're clicking so well. Maybe this is a God thing for Damien's sake.*

Damien turned and looked at her. "Something wrong?"

"No," Jacie said. "Just taking a quick rest." She smiled and started up the trail after him.

The hike took them up the side of the mountain, then down into a ravine. They crossed seven bridges before they came to a wide spot in the trail. "This is my favorite place to rest," Jacie told him.

"It looks good to me," Damien said, smiling at her. "Are you hungry?" he asked. "I brought lunch."

"Oh good," Jacie said. "I only brought energy bars."

"What did you think I meant by lunch?" Damien laughed at Jacie's embarrassed look on her face. He took off his pack and brought it around front. He set it on the ground and peered into it. He pulled out a small insulated pouch. From that, he brought out two flattened peanut butter and jelly sandwiches. He reached back in for chips and Capri Suns. A Ziploc of Oreos was last.

"This is great!" Jacie said as he handed her a sandwich. "Massive sugar-attack lunch. Where are the napkins?"

"Napkins?" Damien said. "We're hiking."

"I always take napkins," Jacie told him.

"You have to pack them back out. No trash cans in the wilderness, remember?"

"Yeah, and the napkins weigh so much."

They both laughed.

After chatting through lunch they sat on a boulder, feet dangling in the cold Stony Brook, saying nothing, but listening to the water pounding over rocks and splashing up from others. Even though they had talked, Jacie still felt as though she knew nothing about him. He seemed to say everything in such vague ways. He was mysterious, for sure. Elusive.

Their hands barely touched. And then, Jacie felt Damien's pinkie finger drape over hers. It seemed odd that such a tiny touch could capture every sense she had. She lay back on the rock and closed her eyes against the sun. She felt sleepy and warm—drifting. Moments later, the sun disappeared and his lips touched hers. Gently. Briefly. It was soft, fleeting, and then his shadow was gone.

She smiled, his kiss still hovering on her lips and in her thoughts. *Something this sweet can't be wrong*, she thought as she drifted off to sleep.

She woke with a feathery touch on her arm. She opened one eye, then shaded them both with her arm. She looked at Damien. "Hello, sleepy."

"How long was I asleep?"

"Hours. I've been bored out of my mind."

"Funny."

"About twenty minutes."

"You want to go now?"

"Not quite yet. Do you?"

"I could sleep all day."

And then he said nothing.

She watched the water, wishing she could figure out a way to bring up God without making him mad.

He said nothing.

She started picking up rocks and tossing them into the deepest pool to hear the musical sounds they made. She thought about the verse somewhere in Peter that said something about winning someone without any words. *Well, there are certainly no words here.*

He said nothing.

She finally said something. "You are the quietest person I've ever known. Do I bore you?"

The crooked smile crossed his face. "Not at all. I really enjoy your company."

"But you don't talk."

He paused. "No, not really." He looked toward the trail as if he heard something. "But it's okay. I don't need to talk to be happy." He leaned back against the rock.

"STUPID!" Came an angry voice from the trail. "STOP IT! RIGHT NOW!"

chapter 9

"You stupid dog!"

The peaceful moment broken, Jacie and Damien sat bolt upright on the boulder.

The man's words sounded so full of hate that Jacie felt she had been hit with them.

A man rounded the bend, a large retriever of some sort pulling at the end of a leather leash. The man looked as though he'd be more comfortable in a suit than in the new sweats he wore. He seemed unaware that he was being watched.

The retriever pounced, grabbing something in his mouth. The man, stick in hand, struck the dog hard on the head. "Spit it out, you fool dog." The dog didn't let go of the object. The man started hitting the dog on his muzzle. The dog yelped. He swore at the dog.

Jacie felt sick. She wanted to say something to the man, but she was afraid.

Before she could stop him, Damien got up from his place on the rock and approached the man. "Hey," he said, "cool dog."

The man looked startled. "Yeah?" he asked, as he puffed himself up, his chest out.

"What kind of dog is it?"

"Stupid Chesapeake Bay Retriever."

"What'd he do to make you mad?" Damien said calmly.

"He's trying to eat a stick," the man said, exasperated. "I bet it's stuck in the roof of his mouth. He always gets them stuck in the roof of his mouth."

The dog began pawing at his mouth. "See?" the man yelled. "He's just a stupid dog that won't obey." He raised his stick again.

Jacie recoiled as if he were raising the stick against her. *Be careful, Damien*, she thought.

"Hitting him isn't going to dislodge it." Damien crouched on the ground next to the dog, gently stroking his head. He put his finger and thumb at the back of the dog's muzzle. The dog opened his mouth; Damien reached in with his other hand and pried loose the small stick that had gotten stuck at the back of his jaw.

"Well . . . he never let *me* do that."

"Maybe you shouldn't hit him."

The man grumbled and walked off, yanking the dog's leash.

Damien walked casually back to where Jacie was sitting.

"That guy scared me. Didn't he scare you?" Jacie asked.

"Naw. I'm an intimidating teenager—I could explode into violence at any moment." Damien laughed. "Probably thinks I'm packing."

"Would you ever carry a gun?" she asked, afraid of the answer.

He looked disappointed. He shook his head and turned away.

"I'm sorry," she blurted.

He turned his back to her and looked through the trees toward the bend in the trail. "I know," he said softly. Getting up, he went to the edge of the brook and squatted there. He picked up a small stick and began to draw it through the mud. Moments later, he took in a deep breath and looked up into the trees. Jacie could swear he wiped his eye as though wiping away a tear, but that couldn't be right. It was probably just an itch.

She stopped watching him. Spying a lonely blue columbine flower, she jumped off the rock and went over to study it. She loved the brilliant purplish blue and the swept-back shape that made it look as if the bright, open face was jetting through space. She looked at it carefully, mentally kicking herself for not bringing her sketch pad. Columbines were easy to find at high altitudes in the spring, but rare at lower altitudes. Why this one was here, she couldn't figure.

"Let's go," he said.

She nodded, and a hand came down to help her to her feet. She took it, grateful for the chance to touch him again. As they walked, he didn't let go until the trail narrowed.

Somehow she was becoming more comfortable with his silence. He'd chosen to be with her, even if he didn't talk, and that communicated plenty. She felt peaceful, quiet. She knew he sensed when she wanted to stop and absorb what she saw. He simply stopped with her and waited until she was ready to go again. He seemed to understand her need to look at light and shadow, color and form. Most of her friends talked so much and moved so much they blew right past the little things that fed her artist's spirit. When she wanted to stop, they asked her to explain why. She couldn't. Explaining would take away from what she was seeing and soaking in. She hadn't realized until now how important it was for her to have these moments.

Then, out of nowhere, Damien began to speak. "I'm a loner, Jace," he told her. "I don't want to be with anyone at school."

Jacie nodded, hurt and relieved at the same time. She knew with her head that they couldn't be together at school, yet her heart wanted it to be that way.

"There's stuff in my head. It crowds out a lot. It's as though there's no room for people."

Jacie nodded again.

He put his hand on hers, squeezed it, then let go. "I'm not like other people."

Jacie smiled. *I know that*, she thought. *I'm glad you're different*. It wasn't just his eyes. It was all of him—how he dealt with the dog beater on the trail, how he let her cry and hurt without trying to fix it. Even though she didn't really know who he was, the mystery drew her to him. Maybe the biggest mystery was how she could be so much herself around him.

She wasn't always sure who that self was, but she knew it didn't matter when she was around Damien. *I can be one person at one moment, and another the next*, she thought. *When I'm around my friends, I have to be who they think I am. The only person I can't be around Damien is the Christian. I mean, I am the Christian, but I can't talk to him about it.*

As they rounded the last corner by the falls, the majesty of them brought a thought to her. *Maybe God is like Damien*, she told herself. *Unknowable. Quiet. Listening. Tender. Strong.*

With incredible eyes.

● ● ●

Jacie moved through her chores without paying attention to what she was doing. She vacuumed while her thoughts relived the hike. She thought of the sunlight overhead, bleaching out the colors of the trees. She dusted the furniture while remembering Damien's every touch—no matter how minor. She thought of his expressions as he talked and thought. She pictured his body moving up the trail.

Nervous energy kept her cleaning beyond her normal chores. If she didn't quit, her mother would get suspicious. But she couldn't sit still. She had to move. Either that, or lie on her bed and dream.

When there was nothing left to clean, she tried to concentrate on geometry. Instead, she drew pictures of Damien. She drew pictures of the trail. She drew a leaf with Damien's face woven into the texture of the leaf. She drew a girl and boy with Stony Brook as a chasm between them. Finally she put his face into the columbine. It was so absurd, she started laughing.

At 6:00 sharp, her mother gathered up a potluck dish and gave last-minute instructions. "If you go anywhere, leave me a note." She looked at Jacie sternly. "Even if you go to your studio."

"Okay, Mom," Jacie said, wishing she had something more to do besides try to figure out what she was going to do about Damien. "I might go to the studio. I don't know. I feel kind of antsy."

Her mother sighed. "I was hoping you'd stay home and relax for once."

Jacie gave her an exasperated look.

"Okay, okay. I understand," her mother said. "But if it's something really out of the ordinary, call me at Rhonda's, okay?"

"Okay. There's nothing now. I'm sure one of my friends will come up with something."

"I know you guys are really good, but I'd rather you didn't do anything without me here, okay?"

"Yes, Mom," Jacie said, irritated. She knew the rules. She'd never broken them. Yet her mother sometimes made her feel as if she couldn't be trusted.

Jacie's mom kissed her on the top of her head. "See you later, Sweetie."

"Bye, Mom."

The door to the townhouse closed behind her mother.

Jacie flopped onto the sofa, picking up the remote. She pointed it at the television and it came to life. She flipped through the channels just like her father did. She turned the power off and began pacing the floor.

She wanted to see her friends. She wanted to go be excited and tell them all about her day. She especially wanted to tell Solana. Solana's brown eyes would be very large and sparkly, and she would lean forward in her chair, eager to hear every single detail.

Except that it's the motorcycle guy. The guy Solana claimed the moment she said he was cute.

Jacie had already broken the cardinal rule of being a friend. She liked someone her best friend liked. Solana—who could have anyone she wanted, and usually did—had put her mark on Damien. More friendships were ruined over this one breach of the unwritten rules than for any other reason.

Jacie sat on the sofa again and crossed her leg. It bounced up and down like mad. She crossed her arms and frowned, staring at the cold fireplace. If she told Becca, would Becca be mad? Yeah, they'd made a pact. But that was only for the summer so they could focus on their relationship with God. Besides, Becca was starting to talk to Tyler's friend Nate Visser an awful lot. *Nate might have even been at Becca's last night.* Of course, Becca's first question would be, "Is he a Christian?" And Jacie couldn't answer that. She was afraid to answer that. Because what if Damien wasn't a Christian?

It sounded like he wasn't, she reminded herself.

Maybe he was once, she argued. She sighed. *Becca would say that wasn't enough. And I don't want to think about that right now.* No, going to Becca would only open up a whole other place where Jacie wasn't ready to go yet.

Tyler? Could she talk to Tyler?

Sighing, she got up from the couch and went into the kitchen. She opened the refrigerator as if it might have the answer tucked inside some plastic Tupperware container. *No. Tyler's just a guy.* She shook her head. *But he's not just a guy. He's our Tyler. He would tell me anything about guys that I needed to know.*

Of course, Tyler always swore her to secrecy when telling her about the private inner workings of guys. She had the feeling he wasn't telling the complete truth. And even when he did share, she didn't always know what in the world he was talking about. She still felt as if most guys had just crawled out of a cave somewhere—and only because it had started to stink in there.

Tiny ants ran amok inside her. That could be the only explanation for why she felt so jumpy. Going to the studio would be pointless. She'd just waste perfectly good paper by drawing a couple of lines and losing her focus.

Did all girls feel this way about guys? She hadn't felt like this when she'd had a crush on Billy Murray in the sixth grade. Not this bad.

She pulled on the bottom of the ragged, bleach-spattered navy blue sweatshirt she wore for housecleaning. She tucked a wisp of hair into the hastily-made twist on the back of her head. *Tyler. I've got to talk to Tyler.*

She couldn't find the cordless and had to punch the locator button. Following the incessant beeping, she found it under the load of laundry sitting on her bed. Punching in Tyler's number, she caught a glimpse of herself in the mirror and wished she hadn't. She was completely disheveled, unkempt, without makeup after her post-hike shower. Sticking her tongue out at herself, she turned away from the mirror.

"Can I talk to Tyler, please?" she asked Tyler's dad. She always got nervous when he answered the phone. More than once Tyler's dad had been rude to her. She never knew whether he might be angry at someone in the house and take it out on her.

"Yo, Baby," Tyler said. "I've been waitin' all my life for you to call."

"You goof," Jacie said. "You have not. You've been in your garage practicing guitar."

Dead silence.

"How'd you know? Don't tell me you heard it all the way over at your place."

Jacie laughed. "Yeah, Ty. I did."

"Good stuff, huh?"

Jacie knew it was best not to answer that one. "I wondered what you were doing tonight."

"Hanging out with my one and only truest love," Tyler teased.

"Oh. You must mean me, then."

"Actually, I was thinking about Maude on Second Street."

Jacie tipped her head back and laughed. Maude, the bag lady who wandered Second Street all day, had a thing for Tyler. He was very sweet to her and bought her coffee and a hamburger whenever he was down there. "Well, before you see your sweetheart, would you have time for me?"

Before Tyler could answer, Jacie's doorbell rang.

"Wait a sec, Ty. I've got to get the door."

Jacie threw open the front door, wishing at once she'd heeded her mother's warning to never, ever, EVER open the front door without knowing who was there. She gaped like a fish. "Uh, hi," she said, feeling quite unlike the Queen who says everything right and proper at all times.

"Jacie?" Tyler's voice floated up from the phone.

Jacie tried nodding. She tried forcing a smile.

"Jacie, are you okay?" the thin voice cried out.

She stared at Damien, feeling as if she must look like Maude on Second Street.

"JACIE! IS IT A MURDERER? SHOULD I CALL 9-1-1?"

"Hi," she said softly.

"Are you hungry?"

She nodded. It could have been a lie. At that moment she didn't know. Didn't care. If he offered her hummus she would have eaten it.

"JACIE, I'M HANGING UP AND CALLING THE POLICE."

"Who's that?" Damien asked.

"Oh!" Jacie put the phone to her ear. She turned away from Damien and motioned him to come in. She pointed at the sofa and walked into the kitchen. "I've got to go, Tyler," she said quietly.

"Who is it, Jace?"

"Nobody."

"I heard a guy's voice."

"Yeah, a guy. But it's okay."

"What guy? Are you sure he's not a rapist?"

"He's from California," she said suddenly, as if that would make everything all right.

"One of your Dad's friends? Okay, I'll let you go. Call me if he leaves soon and we can go do something."

"Okay," Jacie said, not bothering to correct him.

In the living room, Damien stood and smiled. "I'm sorry. I would have called. I don't have your phone number—it's unlisted."

"You don't have my address either," she reminded him.

"Some things are easier to find." He grinned. "Can I take you somewhere for dinner?"

She nodded. Then she gasped. "I've got to change and leave a note for Mom. Stay here. I'll be right back." She started to run from the room. Then she stopped, grabbed the remote and put it in his hands. "Here. Guys like these."

She started out again and stopped. "You aren't supposed to be here. My mother's not home."

He laughed and put the remote on the old trunk they used as a coffee table. "I'll wait outside."

"I'm so sorry."

"Don't be. It's okay. I'll wait outside."

chapter 10

He took her to dinner at La Baguette, a small, inexpensive French restaurant that had a patio in front where they could eat and watch people walk by on the street. Jacie loved their French onion soup with the crusty, gooey, melted cheese on top. But she forgot it meant the cheese made long, drippy chains from her mouth to the soup bowl. It was okay to eat the stuff around her friends, but really embarrassing to eat in front of a cute guy. While he neatly ate his baked croissant sandwich, she felt onion soup dripping down her chin when the cheese finally let go of the bowl.

At first, Damien didn't say much. He watched the people walking by. And then he'd smile at Jacie. It seemed he tried not to notice her struggles with the cheese.

After a particularly difficult cheese maneuver, Jacie was concentrating on wiping her mouth when Damien said, "I was thinking next weekend, maybe we could go on a hike through the Copper Ridge pass."

Well, at least I didn't gross him out too much, Jacie thought. "I'm going to a youth conference in Denver next weekend." At once she wished she could stuff the words back into her mouth.

"Sounds like a church thing," Damien said, sounding disgusted.

"Sort of. A bunch of kids from churches all over Colorado are coming." She stopped dead. She didn't want to tell him it was to help kids learn how to tell others about their faith.

"So, you like God?" Damien asked.

"Yeah, I do."

"Why?"

Frowning, she racked her brain for a replay that seemed just out of reach. *Great. Here I go again. I know the answer. I KNOW the answer. So why does it always fly away the moment I need it?*

He spoke for her, his voice sounding sarcastic. "He's always there and gives you everything you want when you ask for it, huh?"

Jacie snorted. "Hardly. It's usually the opposite."

Damien raised his eyebrows, looking interested.

"God doesn't always seem to be there when I want Him to be, you know?"

Damien nodded almost imperceptibly. "Is He *ever* there?" he said quietly.

Jacie could feel her pent-up frustrations about God just starting to bubble out—things she didn't think she could talk about with her youth pastor or her friends because if she did, they'd probably all fire her from being a Christian. "He's supposed to be there all the time. But I don't think so."

"He's not," Damien said so softly, Jacie almost didn't hear him. It was as if he were speaking to his coffee, not to her.

I shouldn't be talking to Damien about this. I should be telling him all the wonderful reasons why he should become a Christian. I should tell him about Jesus and salvation and all that.

Instead, other things came out. The honest things she really felt. "I pray like I'm supposed to, using the letters A-C-T-S that someone somewhere must have taught us at camp or something—Adoration, Confession, Thanksgiving, and Supplication. But the answers don't always come. Sometimes they do. And sometimes there's answers, but not like I expected. And sometimes it feels like I'm praying to something that doesn't hear. Like I'm making up the idea that God is there."

"Maybe you are."

"No, I know I'm not. I know that sounds like a contradiction and it doesn't make sense. I know God *is* there. He just doesn't seem to be there all the time. And sometimes it seems He cares about me and sometimes it doesn't. It's not consistent at all. It's frustrating."

Damien looked surprised, but he kept quiet.

"And I'm supposed to pray all the time. And there's verses about God answering if we pray according to His will. But what's *that* supposed to mean? Like I know what God wants. He's God. So I get confused about prayers. Is He supposed to answer or not? Lots of times I pray the way I think God would want me to. And He *still* doesn't answer."

"You expect perfect prayers will result in perfect answers?" Damien asked. There was something in his voice she couldn't place.

"Yeah. I mean, after all, if God made everything perfect, wouldn't my mom and dad still be together?"

"What happened? Do you know?" Damien seemed to relax, glad to change the subject.

"It's a long story," she warned.

"That's okay. I have all the time in the world."

Jacie couldn't believe those words that sounded so corny elsewhere actually made her want to talk. Made her want to tell him anything he wanted to know. Sure, he was trying to move the subject away from God. But since she was blowing that one big time, she might as well follow his lead.

"Mom and Dad fell in love in college. They were quite the item. Partly because Dad's African-American and Mom's as white as they come. They were a striking couple. The interracial thing bothered some people, but not most. There was one thing everyone agreed on—and that's how much they loved each other and that they had to have a terrific relationship."

"Because they were together all the time?"

"No. Because they weren't."

Damien raised his eyebrows.

"People knew they really loved each other because they didn't have to be with each other all the time. They were always respectful of the other person even when the other one wasn't around."

Jacie smiled. "My mom drums that into my head all the time. To find someone that is just as secure in my love when I'm not around as when I am."

She stopped, dumbfounded. The thought zipped through her mind, completely ignoring the subject she was supposed to be on. *Isn't this what God wants? For you to know He is there and you can be secure in His love even when He is silent or it seems He is not around?*

"Good advice," Damien said, pulling her back on track.

Jacie nodded. "They would do community service projects together. They really liked working in the soup kitchen. I guess they'd always go and throw glances at each other across the room. The homeless and poor people loved it."

"So if they were so in love and so perfect for each other . . . "

"Well, that's just it," Jacie explained. "They were in love, but they weren't perfect for each other."

"Why? Because it was interracial?"

"No, it wasn't that." For a long time Jacie had asked her mom that question but had never gotten any answers. For as long as she could remember she'd tried to get her mom and dad back together. Her mom would always tell her it was impossible, but the look in her mother's eyes made her think her mother really wanted that too. Only recently had her mother started to tell her the whole story—as many times as Jacie wanted to hear it. And that was a lot.

"I guess it was because they were right for each other in almost every area. The places where they weren't right for each other were big enough for them to realize that the relationship was *mostly* right, but not *all* right."

"So what happened?"

"They got engaged," Jacie told him, watching people walk by.

"They planned to get married the spring after my father graduated—just seven months away.

"About three months into the engagement, both of them started to realize that their lives were really on different tracks. They were great friends, great partners, great together, but they just wanted different things for their lives. My mother wanted children. My father didn't. Both wanted to travel, but my mother wanted to settle down with kids. My father wanted to live in Europe and follow the art community, living in some of the famous places that spawned great artists. A year in Denmark, a year in Italy, a year in England, and so on."

Damien nodded, not paying any attention to all the people on the sidewalk just feet away from them. "Where do you fit in?"

Jacie felt a stab in her heart. *I don't fit in*, she wanted to tell him. *I wasn't wanted*. But she knew what he meant.

"After my parents got engaged, they started being ... um ..." Suddenly she felt awkward and shy. She could say "sex" around any of her friends—including Tyler. But with Damien it would feel so weird.

"Having sex?" Damien offered.

"Yeah. They figured they were getting married, so it didn't matter if they started that part sooner than the wedding. No big deal, you know?"

Damien nodded.

Jacie sighed, and sipped her iced tea. "Mom figures I happened the last time they were together. Right before they broke up." Jacie felt it again—the heaviness that felt like tears, the ugly stuff that took up all the space inside her chest. It came every time she thought about how close she came to not existing. And how her parents really didn't want her. And how it was just a matter of one choice.

Damien reached across the table and put his rough hand on hers. His fingers moved gently across hers, stroking them. He patted her hand and withdrew his.

She swallowed. She stared at her smoothie and tried not to cry.

The moment stretched into many moments. Damien didn't try to force her to talk or force her to not cry. He didn't look at her, but watched the people on the street.

"They didn't stay together because they knew they could always be best friends, but they couldn't always be married." Jacie sighed and stared at her hands. "Mom didn't even tell Dad she was pregnant."

"Why not?"

"She didn't want him to think he was being manipulated into coming back. He didn't know until after I was born and a mutual friend got mad at Mom for not telling. So the friend told my father."

"What did he do?"

Jacie smiled. "My dad came running. Mom says he scooped me up into his huge arms and he was instantly 'gone' over me."

"So he wanted kids after all?"

Jacie shook her head. "No. But he wasn't about to let his little girl go without a daddy. He even begged my mom to marry him. But she refused. She didn't want him to feel tied down to something he never wanted."

"Do you see him much?"

"No—but only because Mom moved us to Colorado to be near her parents. Dad's really good to me. I'm glad he's my dad. I just wish he and Mom could have seen a reason to stay together."

"Do they still get along?"

"Sort of. The whole thing broke both of them, I think. It damaged their friendship somehow. So they're nice and respectful to each other, but I don't see anything left of what Mom says was there." She sighed.

"You still wish?"

She nodded. "A part of me wants what should have been. He's married now . . ."

"With kids?"

"Nope. Just me. And I can see he would never have done well with kids. He's too free-spirited."

"Did he travel through Europe?"

"Yeah. I didn't see him much when I was a little kid. My mom didn't want me traveling so far alone. And I wasn't really the kind of kid who could have. He came to see me a couple of weeks every summer. But . . ." her voice trailed off.

"It wasn't the same, was it?"

She shook her head.

After a long silence, Damien spoke. His words surprised her, because they revealed a rare glimpse of his own life.

"My parents split when I was ten. I've lived with my dad since then." Damien shrugged. "Even when he was home, he wasn't home. He was so busy trying to make a living."

He paused. "Once Mom took off, we hardly ever heard from her."

"Who do you live with here?"

"My dad's sister."

"Why didn't you want to come out here?"

Damien looked at her as if hunting for something. He shifted in his chair. He sipped his coffee. He looked at his watch. "Are you ready to go?"

Jacie frowned at him, confused. She looked at her smoothie that was only half gone. "I guess so." She wanted to ask him the question again.

"Want to go to a movie? The old theater downtown is having a fun movie festival. They're playing *The Princess Bride*."

"I've never seen it. But Tyler is always quoting from it."

"Then you must have your world expanded." He stood, reaching for her hand.

● ● ●

"That was so fun," Jacie told him as they left the theater.

"You liked it?"

"Yeah. I'm going to have to get my mom to see it. She'll love it."

"You laughed at all the right places."

"How could I not?"

"I think it's the fun lines and spoof that make people watch it over and over."

"I know I would watch it over and over."

Damien nodded. He put his arm around her shoulder. "Cold?"

"A little."

He pulled her closer. She wanted to lean into him, lay her head on his shoulder, put her arm around him. Instead, she walked, almost stiffly next to him. *God. I really like him. I want to lean into him. Would you get mad if I did? I want this to be okay with you.*

He looked down at her. "You're so easy to talk to."

Jacie laughed.

"Why are you laughing?"

"If I'm so easy to talk to, why don't you ever talk to me?"

"But I do talk to you."

"It's okay that you're quiet a lot of the time. I know some people are just different from me."

"I like to be quiet. I observe more."

"You also don't have to let anyone inside," Jacie said.

Damien shrugged, but didn't say anything.

"Why don't you trust me?" Jacie asked, her heart racing.

"I trust you."

"No, you don't."

"Yes, I do."

"I know you don't trust me because you won't tell me why you're out here, why you left California, and why you don't live with either of your parents."

"No one cares about that."

They stopped at the motorcycle. Jacie tried to look into his eyes, but he avoided her gaze. "*I* do."

"It's not a big deal, Jacie," Damien said, his voice taking on an icy edge.

Without thinking, she blurted, "What did you do that was so bad that you had to be shipped out here?" When she saw the pain shoot through his face, she felt horrible. *Am I EVER going to learn to watch my mouth?* She wanted to kick herself, crawl into a hole, and take it back.

Damien hopped onto the bike and kick-started it with more intensity than it needed. The bike running, he just sat there without looking at her. With tears in her eyes, she climbed behind him for the silent ride home.

chapter 11

When she opened her locker, she saw a piece of folded notebook paper that perched oddly on top of her books. It looked as if it had been stuffed through the vent. Her name was written on it in unfamiliar writing. She took it, then walked down the hallway to a corner away from the crowds. She leaned against the wall and opened the note.

> *I know you didn't mean it.*
> *Can I see you tonight?*
> *Dinner at someplace really special—like Take-o Taco?*
> *Meet me five minutes before passing bell.*
> *Second period.*

Relief flooded her. Her stupid comment wasn't going to ruin everything. A smile flitted across her face. Folding the note, she put it into her back pocket. She ripped a piece of paper off the bottom of a returned homework assignment and scribbled YES! on it. After she stuck it through the vent in his locker, she went to her first period class. She could hardly pay attention during class, looking often at the clock. At five minutes before the bell rang, she raised her hand and asked to be excused. She slipped through the door and started walking toward the main hall. She rounded the corner and heard a whisper.

"Jacie." Damien's soft voice spoke. "Over here."

She felt the pull on her arm as she was gently tugged into an alcove where a classroom door had once been. He nudged her back up against the sealed door. "Jace," he said, looking into her eyes. "You're making me crazy." He propped himself up by placing his hand on the wall next to her head.

She smiled, and looked shyly toward the floor. "I'm sorry."

He put his finger under her chin and lifted it up. Without warning, he placed his lips on hers. *I can't do this*, she told herself, giving in to the kiss. Returning it. *Becca. I promised Becca I would be careful.* The thought didn't stop her.

A bell rang. The hallway filled with students. Jacie pulled away from Damien. "Melting?" he asked her. She nodded, embarrassed.

"Hannah!" Jacie heard Tyler say. "Where's your next class?" She froze. She tried to make herself smaller, her heart beating wildly. "You want me to walk with you?"

Tyler. He was just on the other side of Damien. If he saw her now, she would be dead. Totally dead.

"What's wrong?" Damien asked.

She tilted her head, barely looking at him. "Someone I don't want to see," she whispered.

Damien looked over his shoulder, watching Tyler move out of sight. "Old boyfriend?"

Jacie shook her head. "We'd better get to class," she said, moving around him and away from Tyler.

"This is more fun," he teased.

"Come on!"

"Mine's right over there," he said, pointing beyond the corner.

"Oh, yeah." She still felt off-balance from the kiss.

"I'll see you later."

"Okay."

Jacie moved down the hall, oblivious to everything and everyone around her.

● ● ●

"What are you working on?" Solana asked, digging into a foil-wrapped burrito.

Jacie shrugged. She studied a group at the table next to them, then drew on her sketch pad. "A lot of things."

"No," Becca clarified. "What are you working on for the contest?"

"What contest?" Hannah asked. She wiped egg salad off her lip, especially careful to tend to the corners of her mouth.

"Art contest," Solana told her. "Well?"

Jacie picked at her tuna sandwich. She really didn't like tuna much, but it was either that or peanut butter and jelly, and she'd had a lot of those lately. "I guess I'm working on a charcoal of your horses, Solana."

Solana grinned. "The *puro tesoros?*" she asked, referring to the wild horses in the mountains that she tracked and befriended, calling them pure treasures.

"Yep."

"She'll win," Solana announced. "She couldn't have chosen more perfect subjects."

"Ever get those eyes right?" Becca asked.

"What eyes?" Jacie asked, knowing exactly what she meant. And no, she hadn't gotten them right. They were closer now. Much closer than before. Now she could see those eyes any time she wished to pull them into her imagination.

"Of that guy."

"Oh," Jacie said. "No. I didn't."

"Are you good enough to win a big prize?" Hannah asked, her blue eyes wide. "I really wish I could see some of your work."

"NO!" The three girls chorused.

"I'm not sure if I'm going to enter the contest anyway," Jacie said, flinching before the expected reaction came.

"You will, too," Becca said. "If I have to break into your studio and take your work and enter it myself, I will."

"And I'll help her," Solana said.

Hannah put up her hands. "Don't you think Jacie should decide for herself?"

Jacie smiled at the support from an unexpected source. "Thank you, Hannah."

Becca dropped her sandwich onto her paper bag, and turned to Hannah. "I can't believe *you* would say that."

"Why?" Hannah asked, her eyes and mouth all innocence.

"Because you, being a Christian and believing the Bible, would know that God has gifted everyone and wants us to use those gifts."

"Is she gifted?"

Solana rolled her eyes and slammed her burrito down on the table. "Yes! She's gifted."

"Don't talk with your mouth full," Tyler said, approaching the table. "Didn't your mother teach you anything?"

"She doesn't think Jacie is gifted!" Becca defended, pointing at Hannah.

"I didn't say that!" Hannah interrupted.

Tyler perched on the edge of the table. He ran his fingers through his hair. "What *did* you say?"

"I didn't say she *wasn't* gifted; I just *asked*."

"Have you seen any of her work?"

"No! They won't let me." Hannah sounded like she was pouting.

Tyler turned to Becca. "If she hasn't seen any of Jacie's work, how can she know?"

"She's supposed to believe us," Solana grumbled.

Jacie put up her hands. "Look, guys, it's okay. It's certainly not worth fighting over." She turned to Hannah. "I can draw some," she said, eliciting snorts from her friends. "All right, better than some. But I'm really not that good. I want to get so much better."

Becca smacked both hands on the table. "And *that's* why we want you to enter the contest and go to the conference!"

A motorcycle roared into the parking lot. Without thinking, Jacie jerked her head up. Some stoner had a tattooed girl on the back of his pathetic Kawasaki bike. She looked away, her heart skipping a beat.

Becca waved her hand in front of Jacie's face. "Hello? Are you in there? We were saying how important it is for you to go to the National Art Conference."

Hannah looked at her. "Is this really important for you?"

As much as Hannah's naïveté sometimes bugged Jacie, there was still something so sincere in her. Jacie loved a tender, sincere heart and she wanted to encourage Hannah's. She looked straight into Hannah's eyes. "Yes. This is the most important thing that could happen." At once she knew her choice of words was wrong.

"Even more important than sharing your faith?"

"No, Hannah," Jacie said, trying not to sound exasperated. "But it is very important to my art—to the gift I think God has given me."

"So why don't you just go?" Hannah said in her perky voice.

"I don't have the money," Jacie said. "That's why these guys want me to enter the art contest. If I got a big enough prize, or several little ones, I might be able to go to the conference."

"Oh," Hannah said. "I'll have to pray about that." She reached into her purse and took out a small, black-and-white-mottled notebook. She opened it and dug around some more in her purse and found a pen. Her face bunched together in concentration.

"What's that?" Solana said, trying to read over her shoulder.

"My prayer notebook," Hannah said. "I don't ever tell anyone I'll pray for them and not write it down. I hate to admit it, but sometimes I forget that I've told someone that. And that's so mean to tell them I'll pray for them, then forget."

Why is it that whenever I'm around Hannah I feel guilty about everything? Jacie thought.

Another motorcycle roared into the parking lot. This time, without looking, Jacie knew it had a purplish-blue gas tank with a white bubble and raised silver letters that said, *Harley.* Her heart thumped wildly inside her. The motorcycle revved in greeting. The rider barely lifted his hand off the handlebars to wave at her. Not a real wave. Just a lift of the hand. His chin jerked up.

"Who's that?" Tyler asked. "Cool bike."

"That's the guy who ran us off the road!" Solana said. "Hey!" she yelled, waving her arms wildly.

"It looked like he was waving at you, Jacie," Tyler said.

Jacie turned to look behind her. "Don't you think he was waving at those guys over there?" She moved her hand in a way she hoped looked to Damien like she was returning his subtle wave, and to the others like she was gesturing to the guys behind them.

Everyone turned and looked. Sure enough, a group of rowdy guys were punching each other and shouting stuff at the guy on the bike.

While everyone else's attention shifted, Solana caught Jacie's gaze and looked steadily at her. Studying her. Jacie didn't know what to do. Smile? Would that make her even more suspicious? If she looked away, that would say the same thing. So she raised her eyebrow. "Guess I'd better get to fifth period."

"Wait a sec," Tyler said, staring at the boy as the bike moved to a parking space. "I've seen that guy before—I know I have."

Jacie swallowed.

"Where?" Solana asked.

Tyler continued to stare. "I think I saw him near Raggs by Razz downtown. If it's who I think it is, he's one of those James Dean kind of guys. A tough guy."

"Introduce me!" Solana said, looking directly at Jacie. "Just my type."

"He gave some girl a kiss when I saw him, so I bet he's taken, Solana," Tyler said.

I hope he didn't realize it was me that guy was kissing, Jacie thought.

"Hasn't stopped me before," Solana bragged.

"How do you know it was him if he was kissing some girl?" Becca asked.

"I noticed him because he has a real distinct leather jacket. I saw him later at the Copperchino down the street. He came in and ordered—"

A mocha latte.

"—a mocha latte."

"A sissy drink," Solana said, disappointed.

Hannah shivered. "He looks so rough. Doesn't he frighten you?"

Solana tipped her head back and laughed. "The rougher he looks, the more interesting the relationship." Solana looked at her friends and their disapproving faces. "Well, within reason. Anyway, he looks like my type."

"So true," Jacie forced herself to say, then her mind screamed, *Stay away from him!* But maybe it was true. Maybe Damien really *was* more Solana's type.

● ● ●

Jacie tried on six outfits before settling on a pair of low-cut jeans and a brick-red sweater that hung just over her belt. She braided a few strands of hair and tied them back with a red ribbon. After turning in front of the mirror four times, she decided to touch up her mascara, then went into her mother's room and misted herself with the perfume, Happy. And she still had a half hour before she was to pick up Damien at school. They'd e-mailed and decided since Jacie had the car, she'd pick him up for their casual evening.

She sat on her bed and stared at her Bible. She picked it up and flipped it open to the Psalms. The words floated around in her head, not connecting with each other. She closed it and put it back on her nightstand. She grabbed a pen and her journal, flopping on her bed.

> I am not cut out for the double life. I swear, today was completely nerve wracking. Why am I doing this to myself? I don't know. Maybe it's because I'm so afraid that Becca and God and people like Hannah would get mad at me. Would they tell me to dump Damien? Probably. I doubt that he's a Christian—well, really, how would I know? In the two times we've talked about God, he's

gotten really mad. So I haven't really asked him. I keep telling myself I should ask. But then, what if he's not? Then I'm sure I would have to turn away from the best thing I've ever had.

I'm so mixed up about this. I know God should be my everything. I should seek Him first. But God doesn't have skin on. I can't see God's eyes. I can't see Him laugh—if He does laugh. I can't hear His voice. I can't feel His touch, and oh how I want to be touched! Do people really understand what it's like to go day after day after day without being touched? I don't think they realize how huge that hole can get. Becca's dad hugs her all the time. Huge bear hugs. And Solana's dad acts all funny and insecure around her. But Solana has all these guys hugging her all the time, touching her, competing for her attention. My mom hugs me sometimes. But she's gone a lot, tired a lot, and I feel so stupid asking her for a hug. I'm supposed to be growing up and figuring out how to deal with that myself.

So if I tell my friends about Damien, I'll have to give him up. And I love talking with him. There's something mysterious about him. Some hurt deep inside. I wonder if he sees the hurt in me, too. We haven't talked about it, but I think we both know it is there. And, unlike God, Damien laughs, and has expressive, beautiful eyes, and he has a voice I can hear and respond to.

But what do I do? I want to do what is right. But I want to be with Damien. Is he really so wrong?

That's the story of my life. Knowing what I should do, and not being able to do it. I'm so sick of failing at everything. The worst is that I think I'm failing God. I mean, here I'm supposed to be a Christian and I'm not doing anything that He wants me to. As soon as I say that to myself, I freeze, knowing that part of all that is the one thing I don't want to give up—Damien. I also know that I don't want to do what I'm supposed to do. I get so scared.

So what do I do about this double life? I don't know . . . keep living it until I figure it out, I guess.

She closed her journal and stuffed it underneath her mattress.

chapter 12

Jacie looked in the rearview mirror one more time, checking her teeth for wayward food particles or lipstick smudges. She pushed at her hair, then drove into the school parking lot. Zipping through the near-empty lot, she rounded the administration building. There Damien leaned against the motorcycle, his arms crossed. His face went from solemn to grinning as she approached.

Jacie stopped her car behind his bike. She shut the car off and took the keys from the ignition before climbing out. "Hey," she said.

"Hey," he said back. He opened his arms and she moved in for a hug. Her face smushed against the soft, black leather of his jacket. He kissed the top of her head. "Ready for the best tacos on the south side of Copper Ridge?"

She laughed. "They happen to be the only tacos on the south side of Copper Ridge."

"That's the only reason why they're the best."

She smiled up at him, teasing. "So why am I so fortunate to be going out to one of the cheapest fast-food places in the entire town?"

"No money," Damien said without apology. "I figured you didn't care where we went."

"You're right." She put her car keys in his hand. "Here. You drive. From what I hear guys have this thing about being in control."

He blanched. "No, that's okay. You drive." He held the keys out to her as if they were covered with poison.

She would have teased him, but he obviously wasn't kidding. "All right," she said softly. She took the keys back. She could have sworn his hand was trembling. But he didn't give her time to be sure. He stuffed his hands into his jacket pockets and jerked his chin up. "Let's go."

● ● ●

Jacie glanced at Damien, then back at the road. "You really love your bike, don't you?"

A sly grin crossed his face. He leaned back against the headrest and gazed at Jacie. "It's not my bike."

"Did you steal it?" she teased.

A dark look flashed across his face. "Yeah. I'm on the lam," he said dryly. "I stole it in California and rode it all the way here without ever getting stopped."

Jacie playfully slapped his arm.

"It's my uncle's."

"And he trusts you with it?"

"Naw. I just take it when he's not looking."

They both laughed.

"I don't know if he trusts me or not," Damien continued. "He just doesn't want to have to drag me everywhere, and neither does my aunt. So, I'm allowed to use it whenever I want—on pain of losing my arms if I hurt it in any way."

"All the guys at Stony Brook are jealous of you, you know."

"*All* the guys? You know *all* the guys?" He seemed to be holding back a smile.

"Of course. And they all confide in me."

Jacie's acceleration from the next stop sign was a little less than smooth. "Maybe you should get a bike," Damien suggested. "Less of a chance of giving your passengers whiplash."

"Yeah, then I'd just dump them off the back."

"But a bike is a whole lot better than a car, don't you think?"

"Yeah, if you like getting soaked in the rain."

"I've heard there's not much rain around here anyway." He looked out the window. "I miss the wind in my face."

"Roll down the window."

He did, then stuck his head out.

Jacie laughed. "You look like a dog."

Damien stuck his tongue out and panted, then sniffed the air. He drew back into the car and leaned over to her. He began snuffling at her hair exactly like her grandmother's poodle. "Stop it!" she shrieked.

He backed up, his eyes dancing with laughter.

I don't understand him, Jacie thought. *One moment he's acting weird about driving a car. The next minute he's acting like a dog and laughing. I don't get it. What I really don't get is how a guy who loves riding a motorcycle can be weird about driving a car? Motorcycles are far more dangerous.*

● ● ●

The rest of the week, Jacie tried to focus on her schoolwork. Every time she picked up a pen she doodled and drew, then scribbled it all out. She tried to prepare herself for the *Brio* evangelism conference by praying more. But every time she closed her eyes, she saw Damien's.

She found she was taking out her journal more often.

> I'm having trouble concentrating. I want to ask someone—my mom maybe. "Have you ever wanted a boy so bad you could taste it all day long? Have you ever wanted him so bad that it was all you could do to get your homework done because he was the only thing you could think about?"

> But of course I won't ask her.
>
> I think about every look that Damien has ever given. I think about every touch. I find myself hoping for a moment when I could accidentally brush up against him—but I haven't even seen him. These are feelings I love and I hate. I hate them because they're all I can think of. I love them because it's so wonderful to remember them all.

Jacie put the pen down and picked up her Bible and the list of verses they were to read and memorize if they could. John 3:16. Romans 5:8 and 6:23, John 14:6, 1 John 1:9. As she read them, thoughts of Damien jumped around, mingling with the verses. She'd take out her journal again, hoping that dumping the thoughts on paper would get rid of them. It seemed to work for a little while. *It's a good thing I memorized all these as a kid*, she thought. *All I have to do is refresh a little.*

On Wednesday night she skipped her own youth group to go to the one for kids going to the *Brio* Faith Fest. There she and her friends met other kids going on the trip. Hannah introduced them to those she knew, and they introduced Hannah to the ones they knew. The night was filled with worship and prayer for the upcoming weekend.

The enthusiasm of the students was contagious.

The evening started Jacie thinking. *Maybe this isn't such a bad thing. Maybe this convention will help give me what I've been wanting—something to help me really share my faith.*

"This is going to be a great weekend," Becca said on their way to the car.

"I'm really excited," Hannah added. "What do you think, Jacie?"

Jacie smiled. "I think so, too. Just what I need."

After she climbed into bed, she reread the verses. This time she recited them easily. *Yeah*, she thought as sleep started to claim her. *This is going to be a good weekend.*

She didn't see Damien the next day or on Friday. She wanted it to be okay, but something in her still ached. She couldn't understand why she felt that way about him. Her growing anticipation for the weekend should be overshadowing her feelings for Damien, shouldn't they?

On Friday afternoon, when she was done packing her duffel, she reached for her journal to throw it on top of her packed clothes. She flipped it open and quickly wrote:

> I think I've become addicted to being able to be real with someone. I like that I don't have to become someone different than who I am. I can relax completely around him, figure out who I am and be that.

Her mom insisted on driving her to Hannah's church to wave good-bye. Jacie hoped no one would think it was dumb that her mother was there. But a lot of other moms were there as well, all waving. Some were a bit too much, shouting, "Be good!" and clinging to their kid as if they were leaving for college, not a weekend in Denver. She was glad her own mother just gave her a quick hug and said, "Learn lots and have a great time."

After a prayer, the bus hissed and lurched. Becca leaned over to Jacie. "Someone drives like you do."

Jacie smacked her.

On the road to Denver, they sang and laughed and talked and threw Chee • tos at each other. She couldn't wait to get there and get started.

chapter 13

Backpacks littered the floors of the hotel lobby—both marble and carpeted. Jacie drank in the lush surroundings, trying to keep her mouth closed. Hannah looked even more struck by the elegant woods, marbles, etched glass, and leather furniture. Jacie wanted to stop at each glass-enclosed display of kimonos and take in the intricate threads weaving pictures of exotic birds, squat, bushy trees, bridges, and mountains. She wanted to stop and sketch the more interesting ones.

Becca grabbed her sleeve and tugged.

Tyler held up his arms, motioning Jacie forward. "Move along, people. There's nothing to see here."

Hannah giggled.

"Nice place," Becca said, nodding her approval. Still, she kept a firm grip on Jacie's sleeve as she maneuvered through the crowd. Jacie felt like a little kid. She would have yanked her arm away, but it was nice to look around and let someone else guide her so she could pay attention to the sights.

Guests not related to the conference peered uneasily at the masses of teenagers throwing Frisbees in the lobby, sprawling on the marble floors playing cards and eating pizza, and stepping over each other without hesitation or forethought.

"Oh!" Hannah gasped. She stared upward. Everyone stopped and followed her gaze.

Jacie suddenly felt woozy. "I'm scared of heights." She grabbed Tyler for support as her head spun.

"But you're on the ground," Tyler said, confused. "Just because it goes way, way, *way* up there . . ." He pointed and waved his arm for emphasis.

"Stop it!" Jacie begged. Her knees buckled.

"I wonder if we're way up there," Hannah said.

Becca snorted. "You guys are such wusses."

"I'm not scared," Hannah protested. "Just amazed."

"I'm scared," Jacie said in a tiny voice.

"I wonder how far up that goes," Tyler said to no one in particular.

"Fifty floors," someone said passing by.

Jacie clapped her hand over her mouth, feeling sick to her stomach.

"We can't afford this," Hannah breathed.

"Special deal," Becca said. "Don't worry. They cram so many of us to a room . . ."

Hannah's youth leader checked the group in and handed out room key-cards. The girls shared a connected room on the tenth floor with four others from Hannah's church, including an adult leader. After moving into their room and going over the ground rules, they went back downstairs to reconnect with Tyler.

Jacie felt a swell of emotions inside. She was excited to be somewhere "adult" without her mother. Not that she didn't love her mother, but it felt so grown-up to be in a hotel without her. On the other hand, she felt like such an imposter. *I can't fool anyone into believing I'm an adult. I'm just a dumb, little, naïve kid.*

Looking at the convention schedule in her hand, she suddenly thought about the art conference. Would she feel she belonged there? Would she feel more or less off-balance than she did here? She was one of five thousand teenagers at this convention—yet she didn't truly feel she belonged. Her friends, meanwhile, seemed to feel totally at home. Hannah lost all her inhibitions, trotting around and saying hello to everyone, introducing herself, and even talking to guests who looked bewildered by the swarming hordes of teenagers.

If I don't feel at home here, why would I feel at home at the art conference? There she'd be the one wannabe out of all the *real* artists. She shook her head to scatter her thoughts. *I'm not going to the conference, so there's no point in thinking about it.*

But she couldn't stop thinking about it. She was supposed to be getting her mind in gear for being with God and listening to Him and learning how to share her faith with others, but all she could think about was being in the middle of a crowd of artists. A hundred of them, to be exact. That was the limit, the brochure had said.

Hannah interrupted Jacie's thoughts, insisting they find a place to flop to look at the schedule.

"Can we please find a place somewhere out of the main lobby?" Jacie asked. "I can't bear to be where we can see all the way up the insides of this place. It makes me shiver."

Tyler ushered them toward the corner of a secondary lobby near the north tower elevators. There, Jacie, Becca, Tyler, and Hannah dropped on the floor, their packs in front of them.

"Look at that guy!" Becca said. She pointed to a man who stared open-mouthed at the kids spilling out of the elevator. He looked flustered at the prospect of attempting to get himself and his luggage inside.

"He doesn't know the rules," Tyler said.

"What rules?" Hannah asked.

"If you don't move quickly, no one will wait for you to get on the elevator."

"Stupid kids," the man muttered under his breath.

Hannah stood. When the next elevator arrived, she moved quickly to the front of the crowd. Once the doors opened, she held up a hand while the elevator's contents spilled into the mix. "Wait a minute! Let this gentleman on, please." The kids all stopped and politely waited for the man to board.

He looked at her without smiling. "I guess not all teenagers are rude."

She flashed him a winning smile. "I'm sorry, sir. You just have to know the rules."

"The rules?" he asked.

By then the elevator had filled in around him and the doors closed.

"Well done!" Becca said.

Hannah smiled and gave a quick curtsey. "Hannah, the Elevator Escort, at your service."

Jacie and Tyler clapped. "Bravo."

"When's our first meeting?" Becca asked.

Hannah checked the schedule. "General session at 7:00."

Tyler checked his watch. "It's 6:30 now."

Hannah gathered the backpack Jacie had given her. "We should get to the Convention Center now if we want a good seat."

Jacie felt butterflies rise up in a cloud in her stomach. Why was she nervous about the session? It wasn't like they were going to have to witness to anyone there. Still, she took a deep breath and forced a smile.

"Onward!" Becca said, leading them through the crowd. They crossed the street in a mass of kids that looked like a herd of cattle forced into a small corral. It was just like the school hallways—without the walls. With Becca's expert skills in crowd-weaving, they found great seats near the front of one of the four sections in the cavernous convention center meeting hall. A round, black stage sat in the center.

"This set-up is different from what I'm used to," Hannah said.

"I like it," Tyler said. "More people can get closer to the stage."

"I just hope we don't have to look at someone's back the whole time," Hannah said, looking around. "Maybe we should find another seat."

"We're fine," Becca said. "If they have video screens facing every direction, I'm sure they've figured out that problem already."

Jacie kept her eyes on the large video screens hovering over the stage. They flashed verses, pictures of kids at school, quick-burst interviews with kids at the conference, and stupid human tricks. The gang talked and laughed, waiting for the meeting to begin. Becca sat on the back of the seat in the row in front of them, her feet on her own chair. "This is too exciting," she said, her eyes scanning the room. "We all believe in Jesus! This is so incredibly awesome."

Jacie wanted to agree with her. It *was* awesome. But something was missing. She didn't dare be the one dissenting voice. She would just sound like a whiner or a crab. And she couldn't put her finger on what was wrong, anyway.

● ● ●

Numbers burst onto the video screens, lively music filling the air. "TEN!" students began to shout. More joined in, following the countdown on the screen. "NINE! EIGHT!" Becca jumped from her perch. The others stood with her. "FIVE! FOUR!" Jacie felt the corporate energy surging through her. Her heart beat faster.

"TWO! ONE!"

The sound of people clapping to the music pulsed through the room. The popular band, Kerygma, ran onto the stage, its music loud and throbbing. Overhead lights dimmed, and spotlights split streams of colored light all about the auditorium. Fog machines hissed and the fog turned colors.

The band played its most widely known song. Becca, Tyler, Jacie, and even Hannah joined everyone else in singing along. Hannah leaned over to Jacie and shouted, "Now I can tell all my friends I sang live with Kerygma."

Jacie smiled. This Hannah was so unlike the school Hannah. This Hannah sang at the top of her lungs, clapping to the music and shrieking and waving her arms with everyone else when the song was over. This Hannah moved to the music—very well, Jacie thought. This Hannah talked eagerly to the kids around her. Jacie leaned toward Becca's ear. "Where did the shy, timid girl go?"

Becca shrugged. "I like this girl a whole lot better!" she yelled back.

Jacie nodded.

Tyler grinned, pointing at the band, then at himself, then back at the band. Becca and Jacie nodded, faking smiles. "When's he going to get it?" Becca asked through clenched teeth.

"I don't know."

Tyler continued singing loudly and off-key.

"At least he puts his whole heart into it," Jacie whispered back to Becca. Becca watched Tyler for a moment, then smiled.

The band played a few more rousing songs, Tyler strumming an air guitar and playing imaginary drums.

"He's really good like this," Becca said.

Jacie laughed.

When the band slowed down to quieter worship songs, Hannah closed her eyes. She reached her hands high, swaying to the music as she sang.

God? Are You really here? Jacie prayed silently. *I know we aren't supposed to go by feelings. But something is happening. Something that makes me think of You. Makes me want You. Makes me want to give You everything I have.*

Jacie closed her own eyes and bowed her head as she sang. She bowed her whole heart before God. She could imagine herself at the foot of a throne, her head low, singing this song of worship. The song filled her, moved through her—and, she hoped, on toward God.

Then came announcements. A skit. Kids sharing. A speaker.

Jacie sat riveted through it all. She felt as though she'd come home. She felt as though she were the only person in the room, yet not alone because there were thousands of others who were there for the same reason. They were there because they loved and believed in a God who provided salvation—a way out of the messes they'd gotten themselves into and would get themselves into. It helped her feel stronger, braver. As if she wasn't alone in this.

Even witnessing didn't seem quite so scary anymore.

• • •

After the session, they went to their rooms. When they finally turned off the lights and stopped talking and giggling, her thoughts drifted to Damien. She missed him so much. She couldn't understand why she missed him at all. It wasn't like Damien was with her all the time. It wasn't like they were boyfriend and girlfriend. She could never expect they would be. He was different. Elusive. Even if he was a Christian, he was certainly mad at God.

In spite of that she couldn't get rid of her strong feelings for him. She thought of his gentle touch—his hand on the small of her back when she'd been crying. His pinky finger reaching out for hers on the boulder. His hands on her shoulders as he looked into her eyes. His hand reaching for hers in the movie.

If she'd been anywhere else, she'd be embarrassed at thinking about these touches. But in the dark, in the queen bed, with Becca moving to get comfortable next to her, she could indulge to her heart's content.

• • •

"Wasn't that guy great?" Hannah asked as the girls stood and stretched. "I took so many notes."

"Yeah, he was good," Becca said.

"They've all been good," Jacie added. All day she'd been doodling and taking notes in the seminars. The teachers made sharing her faith sound so easy and so within her grasp. They were so interesting, she only thought of Damien when she thought of how she could take what she learned and share her faith with Damien.

"I wonder where Tyler went," Becca said, looking around.

"He took off with the guys. They're going to gorge on pizza."

Hannah bounced about. "I'm so excited! Tomorrow we'll get our assignments and we'll get to go out and talk to people. Do you think you're ready, Jacie?"

"As ready as I'll ever be."

chapter **14**

"We're assigned to the mall," Hannah said, her face flushed with excitement. She rolled and twisted her hair, popping it onto the back of her head, holding it there with a toothy clip. She smoothed her corduroy skirt and made sure her cream blouse was tucked in just right all the way around.

Becca rolled her eyes. "Great. We can shop and witness at the same time."

Jacie forced a laugh. "Good thing Solana isn't here." Suddenly all the bravado she'd felt inside the convention center vanished. It was as if her bravado had all the substance of cotton candy.

"I was hoping we'd be assigned to The Great Indoors," Becca teased.

Tyler grinned. "Yeah! Basketball and witness—the perfect combination." He turned to Jacie. "Are you feeling better about this?" he asked.

Jacie looked to see if Becca and Hannah were watching for her answer. They were. "Oh, sure," she said, hoping God would know she was being sarcastic, and that the others would think she was being serious. She wished she could be serious. She took a deep breath and said, "This is going to be really good. It's going to be fine."

"You want to go with me?" Tyler asked her.

"She's going with me," Hannah said brightly. "I think the two of us will make an effective team."

Jacie opened her mouth to protest, but nothing came out. She closed it and smiled. Really, who better to learn from than the best?

"Fine!" Becca said, grabbing Tyler's arm. "Let's go."

Tyler shrugged and followed Becca.

Jacie watched them walk away as though they were abandoning her.

"This is so exciting," Hannah said. "Five thousand teenagers, spread out all over Denver. Just think of how God's Spirit is going to be moving today."

Jacie tried to picture it, and couldn't.

"Let's go to the food court," Hannah said. "That's where people are—"

"Captive audiences?" Jacie said, wishing she could stuff the words back into her mouth.

"No! It's where they're relaxed and not rushing to another store. They're more willing to talk."

●●●

They moved through the crowds, past the waterfall and up the stairs toward the food court. Jacie's heart beat faster as she looked into the people's faces. They didn't look eager to be talked to by a stranger about anything, much less about Jesus. Her stomach flipped a couple of times. She licked her dry lips.

Hannah practically pranced. Her hands fluttered and she smiled happily at everyone they passed. "Do you want to go first?" Hannah asked, excitement driving her voice and energy up.

Jacie gave her another fake smile. "No. You go ahead. You're obviously anxious . . ."

"Yes! How could you tell?"

Hannah circled through the food court, scanning the people and the layout and muttering softly to herself. Jacie wasn't sure, but thought Hannah might be praying. Jacie trailed her, trying to follow her gazes. *God*, she said silently, *Maybe you can help me learn something from her*. Her stomach did another flip.

Hannah picked up her pace. It seemed she was headed for a mother struggling with three young children and a tray laden with food.

"Hi," she said to the mother. "It looks like you need some help." She reached for the tray.

"Oh, thank you," the mother said, returning Hannah's smile and letting her take the tray.

"My name's Hannah, and this is Jacie."

"I'm Sue," the woman said. "And these are Eric, Nathan, and Emily."

Jacie snagged a high chair and put it by the table Sue had chosen near the giant stone fireplace. Sue slipped Emily into the chair while Nathan slugged Eric. Eric punched Nathan back.

"Boys!" Sue said. "Stop it right now."

"Thanks for rescuing me," Sue told Hannah. "I don't think anyone has ever offered to help me before."

"No problem," Hannah said. "We all need rescuing at some time or another."

"Now that's sure the truth."

Jacie tried to keep the boys occupied by playing with the dinosaur toys that came inside their lunches. She hoped it would excuse her from actively participating in the conversation.

"I was even rescued from death!" Hannah said.

Sue's eyes grew wide. "Really?"

Jacie cringed.

"I was so grateful that I pledged my life to the One who saved me."

I would never feel comfortable saying that. Jacie made the dinosaurs dance together, resulting in sniggers from the boys.

Sue opened a squat jar and shoveled some yellow, squishy stuff into Emily's open mouth. Emily's arms and legs flapped up and down every time she swallowed. "I would, too," the woman said. "Wow."

"You can, you know," Hannah said.

Jacie trembled.

The woman looked at her quizzically. Emily started flapping, her eyes and mouth open wide, focused on the full spoon hovering in the air. "What do you mean?"

Hannah went on to explain all about God's love, Jesus' sacrifice, and the way out of the mess people make of their lives. Sue shoveled and listened, occasionally taking a bite of her own burger or fries dipped in ketchup.

Jacie heard pieces of the conversation as she kept the boys busy with their food and toys.

"I can ride a big boy's bike," Nathan bragged to her.

"No, you can't," Eric said, his dinosaur stomping through his burger. He sucked off the ketchup and bread that stuck to the dinosaur's legs.

"Can too."

"Can not."

"With training wheels I can," Nathan blurted.

"That's really good," Jacie said.

"I could never be what you call a Christian," Sue was saying.

"Why not?" Hannah asked.

"It's too hard." She looked around as if to see if anyone was listening. She leaned forward. "And I'm often not a nice person. When I get tired, or overwhelmed, I get . . . well . . ."

"Grumpy?"

Sue laughed. "My word probably wouldn't be as nice as yours, but, yes, grumpy. Certainly not nice to be around. I make choices I'm not proud of—"

"We all do," Hannah reassured her.

Somehow Jacie couldn't believe Hannah ever made choices she wasn't "proud of."

"And I don't think believing anything is going to change what I am."

"Jesus is changing *my* life."

"Most people I hear talk about God say it in the past tense, but you say it like it's happening now."

Hannah smiled warmly at her. "It is. It's a process. I mess up all the time, but the Bible promises that 'He who began a good work in you will carry it on to completion.'"

"Really?" Sue's eyes filled with tears. "Well, when you put it that way . . ."

A few minutes later, after Hannah had explained more, Sue and Hannah were holding hands and praying. The boys looked at their mother, then at Jacie. "What are they doing?" Eric asked.

"Praying," Jacie told him.

"Why?" Nathan snorted. "That's really dumb."

Jacie knew this was a great moment to tell this little boy about how Jesus loved him, too. She searched her brain for something to say, and nothing was there. It was as if her brain had suddenly turned into a dark cave—huge, cavernous, with only an echo for an answer.

"Thank you," Sue whispered to Hannah. Emily let out a squeal of displeasure, and Sue quickly filled the gap with yellow mush. The arms and legs flapped. Hannah handed Sue a card and a little booklet. "To get you started," Hannah told her.

● ● ●

For the next couple of hours, Jacie was stunned by Hannah's boldness. Hannah would look for someone who might need help, or who might be sitting alone and looking lonely, and approach them with such friendliness that no one turned her down. Some people chatted with her, obviously interested. Some were not interested, but said they'd think about it. She gave all of them a card with a Web site address and a toll-free number they could call to talk more. And three of the eight people bowed their heads right there in the food court to accept God's gift of eternal life through the mercy and sacrifice of Jesus.

Instead of boosting her confidence, Hannah's successes made Jacie more uncertain than ever.

"It's your turn," Hannah said to Jacie. "We've only got an hour left. I really shouldn't be hogging all the fun."

"I—I—can't," Jacie whispered.

Hannah crossed her arms and looked at Jacie. "Sure you can. You can do all things through Christ who strengthens you."

"I know, I know," she said, her voice still a whisper. "I just feel frozen. Stuck."

"God isn't a liar, is He?"

Tears came to Jacie's eyes. She shook her head.

Hannah grabbed both her hands and bowed her head. Jacie bowed her head, but didn't feel much like praying to the God who was making her do this scary thing. Instantly she felt bad about *that* thought.

"God," Hannah said in a voice that seemed way too loud. "Please help my sister Jacie to see that You will give her everything she needs to accomplish Your will. And since Your will is for all Your children to share Jesus with the lost, You will help her to do it. In Jesus name, amen!"

Jacie lifted her head. Hannah looked at her with the expression her mom wore when she couldn't fathom Jacie's emotions. "You're shaking," Hannah said, sounding amazed.

"I can't help it."

"Yes, you can. Just let go and let God do the work."

Jacie dropped her head and took a deep breath. A tear fell. She hoped Hannah didn't see that. She hated her fear. She hated that Hannah made her feel like a bad little girl. She hated that she couldn't be who God wanted her to be.

She swiped at her face, hoping it looked as though she was simply moving the hair out of her face. "Okay. Let's go."

Jacie felt her insides scramble.

chapter

Somehow, in a matter of seconds, it seemed she'd traded her boots in. Her new ones had magnets on the bottom. Or lead in them. Or she needed new feet. She tried to scan the food court and make some sense out of it. But the images weren't registering. She moved to the fireplace and sat on the huge hearth.

"What are you doing?" Hannah asked.

"Thinking."

"You shouldn't be thinking. You should be praying and acting."

Jacie nodded. Hannah was right. But she couldn't get her mind in gear to pray anything more than, *God, oh God, oh God, help me.*

She took a deep breath and got up, then followed a man who had a couple of little kids in tow. "Hi," she said. "Do you need help?"

He stopped. He looked at her. "I don't think so."

"Okay," she said. She walked back to the hearth and sat down. The heat felt incredibly good against her back. She didn't want to get up.

"What are you doing?" Hannah demanded, her hands on her hips.

"I didn't know what to do."

"You could have offered to help anyway, or moved on to someone else. Now get up."

Jacie nodded. She took a deep breath and held her head up. *I WILL do this. I will!*

At that moment, an elderly couple sat at a table close to the hearth. *This I can do*, she thought.

"Hi," she said to them. "How are you folks today?"

The plump old woman smiled at her. "Doin' just fine nows we got food and fire. Right, Henry?"

He nodded and smiled. "That's all we need to make us happy anymore."

Jacie smiled back. "That's great." She knew there was something she could connect that to. Something about God. Something about Jesus. Being happy. Content. Yeah, that was it. But what? How could she get the conversation going to where she could talk about their future? What future? Could she really talk about dying with people this old? Wasn't that rude?

"What makes you happy, Honey?" the woman asked, her hand trembling as she attempted to spear some kind of Chinese chicken onto her fork.

"My art," Jacie blurted, immediately knowing the answer was *wrong*.

"Really?" Henry asked. He pointed his fork at his wife. "My Doris here was a pretty good artist."

"Until I lost my steady hand to Parkinson's," she said, holding out a quaking hand to prove it.

"What was your medium?" Jacie asked.

"Watercolor."

"Would I know your name?"

"Oh, no, Honey. I only painted a little bit for family and friends. Nothing special."

"Now, that's not the truth at all," Henry said. "You were really good. You could have sold paintings with the best of them."

Doris blushed.

"Why didn't you?" Jacie asked, truly curious.

"I let things get in the way."

"She didn't believe in herself," Henry said, waving his fork around. "I kept telling her she was good, but she just didn't believe it."

"I had little kids," Doris said. "And Henry's right. He told me and told me to go back to college and take some classes. But I just didn't. I didn't think I could ever be good enough and I didn't want people to laugh at me."

Hannah elbowed Jacie.

"Oh," Jacie said, "I'm sorry. I'm Jacie and this is my friend Hannah."

"Hello, Hannah," Henry said. "I'd shake your hand, but I don't think you want Orange-ee beef all over. That's what the Orientals call it. Orange-ee. I guess they must pronounce all the vowels."

"Hannah!" Doris said. "What a pretty name."

"It's from the Bible," Hannah said, elbowing Jacie even harder.

Conversational doors were flying open all over the place, and all Jacie could do was smile and nod and think of how nothing was coming to her head. *God, help me here! Hello? I need some words here.*

"How nice," Doris said. "I never quite got into the Bible, you know. Too much going on."

"I never tried," Henry said. "Words were too hard. But I've always been a decent kind of man."

Doris reached across the table and patted his arm. "You were always a *good* man, Henry. No need to be ashamed of your life." She turned to the girls. "He never told a lie that I know of. Good to me. Good to the kids. Hardworking. Look for a man like that and you can't go wrong."

Jab, jab, jab. Hannah's elbow seemed to grow barbs.

"Jesus," Jacie blurted. "He loves you." Her face flamed with heat. It sounded so lame coming from her mouth.

Doris and Henry looked at her. The relaxed look on their faces tightened just a little. "Why, of course He does, Honey."

Hannah sighed heavily. "Excuse me," she said, and she walked away.

"Nature calls, eh?" Henry said, winking at Jacie.

"What kind of art are you interested in, Honey?"

"Acrylics. Watercolors. Pastels. Ink."

"You must be good," Henry said.

"Not really."

Doris looked her in the eye. She leaned so close, Jacie could smell the Chinese chicken on her breath. She put her hand on Jacie's arm. "I bet you're good. I bet you have a gift. And I want you to go after it, Honey. Go after it and don't let it go." She patted Jacie, smiled, and moved back into her own space.

Henry winked at her. "She knows what's what, my Doris does. You'd do just fine to listen to her."

Jacie searched her brain for something spiritual, but still nothing came. Instead she answered the questions they asked, asked them about their lives and their family. They laughed. They chatted. But not once could she grasp hold of anything that could remotely be considered witnessing.

"Where's your friend?" Henry asked, looking around.

"I'm not sure," Jacie said, having seen Hannah standing off to one side, scanning the crowd. Since then, Hannah had disappeared from view.

When the couple finished their meal, Jacie took their paper plates, napkins, and empty cups to the garbage. They stood and wrapped their arms around her as though she were a grandchild leaving on a long trip. "You keep painting," Doris admonished her. "I want to see your work some day. I want to say I met her and she's a sweet girl. I want to be able to tell people that, you hear?"

Jacie smiled. "Thanks."

Henry gave her a snug hug, then held her at arm's length. "You just listen to my Doris, hear? She knows what's what."

"Okay," Jacie said, stifling a giggle.

As they walked away, she sat back on the hearth, watching them go. Suddenly words flooded her mind. Words she could have said.

She shook her head, angry at herself. *God*, she prayed silently, *can You send someone else to tell them what I couldn't? They're such sweet people.*

"Jacie."

Jacie looked up. Hannah stood there, looking down at her. "So?" she asked, her excitement restrained. "How'd it go?"

Jacie bit her lip. "They're really nice people."

Hannah's hands flew out, palms up, questioning. "Yeah, and?"

"Well . . . "

"Was it wonderful? I didn't see them pray, but were they open? Did you give them a card? Tell me what you said."

Jacie looked at her watch. "It's 4:00. Time to meet the others." She stood and brushed off the seat of her jeans.

Hannah's face fell. "You didn't tell them, did you?"

Jacie shook her head. "I couldn't." All the sweetness and joy and encouragement Henry and Doris had given her seemed to melt away. She wanted to defend herself, but knew there was really no defense.

"So what did you talk about?"

"Art," Jacie said, shame filling her.

"But—" Hannah said, her voice brimming with disappointment. "You had such an opportunity."

"I know," Jacie almost whispered, weaving through the food court crowd.

"I left because I thought maybe I was making you more nervous. I was hoping you'd relax if I wasn't there staring at you."

Jacie kept biting her lip and moved into the central part of the mall. She tried to see through the blur of her tears and hoped that they wouldn't fall.

● ● ●

A large group of students gathered around the main entrance to the mall. Lots of excited chatter, high-fives, and punches were being exchanged when Jacie and Hannah arrived.

Becca and Tyler practically glowed. "Was that not the best thing ever?" Becca asked.

Tyler ran his fingers through his hair. "We talked to this motorcycle dude—"

"*You* talked to the motorcycle dude. He was almost scary."

"I didn't think you were scared of anyone," Hannah said.

"This guy was extreme," Becca said. "He was *almost* scary."

"He was kind of rude at first," Tyler continued. "But then we got to him. I think he really did mean it when he prayed."

"He prayed?" Hannah asked, excited. "That's wonderful."

"He meant it," Becca said. "It was more than awesome. We spent so much time with him that we didn't have time to talk to anyone else—"

"But I don't think that mattered," Tyler said.

"Of course it didn't matter," Becca said. "He needed the whole time to make a decision." They high-fived each other. Becca turned to the girls. "So, how'd it go with you?"

"God was really working in that food court," Hannah said. "Things were going so well. I had *three* people pray. Can you believe it? It was so amazing." Then her face fell. "But then—" She shook her head, her hair falling from the clamp. She removed the clip and opened it and closed it. The plastic jaws seemed to proclaim Jacie's disgrace.

Becca and Tyler looked at each other, confused. "Why are you upset that God was working?" Becca asked.

Tyler shook his head. "Girls don't make sense," he told them.

Hannah threw up her arms. "I'm not mad, I'm just frustrated and I don't understand."

Becca gave Tyler a look. "No, girls don't make sense. At least not at this moment."

Hannah fidgeted. Her hands moved about as if trying to find the words hanging somewhere in the air—if only she could grab them. "I just don't know what to think. Jacie, I'm not trying to be mean, but—" She sighed and tried again. "An outsider would never know you were a Christian. What happened to the Bible verses you memorized?"

Jacie swallowed and swallowed and swallowed. She ground her teeth, willing herself not to cry.

"Not everyone is open to the truth," Becca said pointedly. She put her arm around Jacie, and the action cut loose the tears.

Hannah squirmed some more, looking sadly at Jacie. "I know that. But that wasn't the problem."

"Then what was?" Becca asked.

Hannah looked at her shoes. It was, Jacie thought, as if she were being forced to tattle on Jacie, but didn't want to. So Jacie decided to tattle on herself and save Hannah the dirty job. "I had a whole bunch of times when I could have said something about God. But I froze." She shook her head. "All we talked about was art."

The furrow between Tyler's brows deepened. "I don't get it. Why is it so wrong to talk about art?"

"We were *supposed* to be *witnessing* to people," Hannah blurted.

"I couldn't do it," Jacie told them as she pulled away from Becca, feeling she didn't deserve comforting. "My brain went empty. I couldn't think of anything to say."

"You seemed to be having a chatty conversation with them after I left," Hannah pointed out. "I was sure you'd finally started talking about your faith."

"Maybe there just wasn't an opportunity to turn the conversation toward God," Becca said, obviously trying to stand up for Jacie.

Hannah turned to Tyler as if hoping to win him over. "While I was sitting there, almost everything they said could have been tied to something biblical. But she didn't pick up on any of them. Not *one*."

Jacie nodded. "She's right. But it was weird. I kept praying for words about God, but nothing came out. Only surfacey stuff." The weird thing, Jacie thought, was that as she recounted the situation, at first she felt awful, but then she felt a wave of peace that left as quickly as it came.

Hannah shook her head. "The *one* thing she said about God was, 'Jesus—He loves you.'"

"That's a good thing to say," Tyler said.

Hannah shook her head. "She said it—like it was a question. Or like if they contradicted her, she'd agree with them."

"Not everyone can do this quickly," Becca said, not sounding quite convinced.

"She's been a Christian her entire life," Hannah said as though Jacie weren't standing there. "I can't understand why she can't or won't do this. It's so easy."

Jacie felt the weight of Hannah's disappointment. It felt like God's disappointment.

Her three friends looked at her, speechless.

Jacie hung her head and walked away. She'd find another way back to the convention. *God, I'm so sorry.*

"Jacie!" Becca called. "Come back!"

"Let her go," Jacie could hear Hannah say. "Maybe she needs some time alone."

chapter 16

Jacie found a city bus and boarded it. Her precious money was swallowed up by the *ka-ching* of the cash box.

She wouldn't have enough to buy dinner. Well, she could have a kid-sized McDonald's hamburger with a cup of water. She made her way to the back of the bus and sat on the aisle end of the seat to discourage anyone from sitting next to her.

Little tears dripped down her face. She did nothing to stop them, nothing to wipe them from her cheeks. *God. I'm so sorry. I'm such a failure. Why in the world would You even want me to be Your child? I can sing with the rest of them. I can make huge claims in a huge room filled with lots of kids. But when it comes down to real life, I can't even talk with nice people like Henry, Doris . . . or Damien. I can't even talk to my dad.*

She stared out the window as the city bus passed the group of excited kids disappearing into vans and church buses. She was supposed to be one of them.

She was on the inside, looking out.

Will I ever be able to share my faith?

The answer came suddenly.

Yes. But not the way you expect.

Jacie turned around. Did someone say something? She touched her hand to her heart.

Peace.

Where did that come from?

Nothing made sense.

But then, for once, it didn't have to.

● ● ●

At the hotel, Jacie stuffed her clothing and toiletries into her duffel. She ignored Hannah's sighs and sideways glances. When Hannah finally spoke, her voice dripped with honey. "It wasn't easy for me at first, either."

Jacie couldn't respond.

"We can set up a time when you can come over and practice. That will help."

Jacie shook her head and looked right at Hannah. "No, thanks."

"Really, it will just take—"

"Give it up, Hannah," Becca said, zipping her duffel. "Leave her alone."

"*Brio* sisses encourage each other to do better," Hannah said. "That's what Susie says. Remember?"

"And sometimes *Brio* sisses know when to let God talk to someone in His own way."

Hannah sighed. She disappeared into the bathroom, the door closing behind her.

Jacie gave Becca a half-smile she knew Becca would understand. They were *Brio* sisses to the max. Even before *Brio*, they'd read each other's faces across the classrooms of childhood. And it grew deeper in middle school and high school when *Brio* came along and gave them things to talk about. Becca would know what her brief look meant. *Everything isn't okay—but it is. I'll be all right.*

There would be a final rally. Jacie didn't know if she'd go or not. She'd throw her duffel into the church bus. Then she'd pick up her kid's burger at Mickey-D's. She might come back to the hotel and look at kimonos. She might draw some. And she might sit in the back row of the rally where the other failures sat.

"Come with us?" Becca asked as the water ran in the bathroom.

Jacie shook her head. "Don't worry. It's not you—" She picked up her things and left the room, handing the key-card to the leader on her way out.

● ● ●

As Susie Shellenberger stood to give her last talk, Jacie put her feet up on the seat in front of her. She rested her head against the cement wall behind her chair. Students filled the seats in front of her. Her friends were in the third row. She'd watched from a distance as they worshiped. She belonged with them—or did she? They were all Susie encouraged them to be—sold out in their faith. Standing firm in all they knew and believed. And here she couldn't even open her mouth to talk to a sweet old couple about anything but art.

She took her journal and a pen from her backpack.

> What's wrong with me? I must be so broken. I want to go to the National Art Conference even more now that I've been to the Brio Faith Fest. The really good part was being with all these girls who read Brio Magazine, their friends, and some guys who read Breakaway, too. It was good—until yesterday. But I shouldn't want to go to something about art. I should want to work harder on learning how to share my faith. What does God think of me? What do my friends think?

● ● ●

Jacie leaned her head against the bus window. She stared without

stuck in the sky

seeing. The bus bumped into the church parking lot. She could see her mother, looking great in jeans and a sweater, standing off to one side—alone, scanning the two buses for her daughter.

A knot in Jacie's chest tightened, and a tear escaped. *At least Mom loves me.* Mom had always been at every school event, praised every piece of artwork. Jacie didn't always appreciate everything her mom did, but right now she felt a surge of gratitude that Mom was always there to meet her. Other kids' moms might be late or crabby or forget altogether. But her mother never did.

When Jacie stepped off the bus, her mother rushed over and gave her a big hug. "Hi, Sweetie."

"Hi, Mom."

"Did you have a good time?"

Jacie shrugged. "The meetings were awesome." She knew she was sending two different messages, but she didn't care. She didn't want to talk about it—even to Mom.

After finding her duffel in the pile of luggage, she threw it in the backseat of her mother's Nissan. Then she sat in the frontseat and stared out the passenger window.

"Do you want to say good-bye to your friends?"

Jacie shook her head. "I'll see them tomorrow," she said flatly.

Without looking, Jacie knew her mother's mouth had gone from soft and relaxed to a stiff line—keeping quiet because Mom knew Jacie didn't want to talk. *Another thing to be thankful for*, Jacie thought. *But I know I'll never tell Mom what happened. I just can't.*

The next morning, Jacie didn't even care what she put on. She just grabbed something and pulled it over her head. She snatched a pair of jeans and slipped them on. Finding a pick, she drew it through her tight black curls, then clipped them just behind her ears. She put on mascara and a little eyeliner, not bothering with blush, shadow, or lipstick.

Her friends would know all of this meant she didn't care. She didn't even care that they'd know.

She felt dead inside. She couldn't be what she wanted to be—or what God wanted her to be. She'd tried, hadn't she? She'd gone to the conference, done all the worship things, taken good notes. There had been moments when she felt she could even become the evangelist. But when the moment had presented itself perfectly, she'd failed completely.

Numb, she drove to school. She went straight to her locker, going the long way around so she'd miss "the" table. She spun the combination dial to the right, to the left, to the right. As she yanked open the door, a flutter of papers fell to her feet. The writing made her heart flutter, too.

There were ten of them—ten little notes. Each had her name on it. Each was numbered.

> #1
> Friday was boring because:
> Jacie wasn't smelling books.
>
> #2
> Saturday morning was boring because:
> There was no one to hike with.
>
> #3
> Saturday afternoon was boring because:
> There was no one to eat smushed peanut butter and jelly sandwiches with.
>
> #4
> Saturday night was boring because:
> There was no one to hold hands with in a movie.
> There was no one to kiss.

Jacie blushed.

> #5
> Sunday morning was ... well, it was the same as always because you are at church Sundays.

#6
Sunday afternoon wasn't boring because I had spent all weekend thinking about you. And I was writing these notes so I was thinking about you again. And I went to Copperchino and smelled a book in memory of you (War and Peace).

#7
Sunday evening was full of energy, wishing I could come see you get in tonight.

#8
Monday morning was really exciting because I knew that somewhere, some way I would see you today.

#9 TONIGHT??
E-mail me time and place!

#10
Or you can pretend none of these notes ever happened.

For the first time since her failure the day before, she felt like she might actually be worth something. At least she was worth something to Damien. His notes lit something inside. She wasn't sure what it was, but the darkness wasn't quite so dark any more. After knowing him only three weeks, she'd found he was a part of her life she couldn't imagine doing without.

She looked at her watch. If she hurried, she could go to the library and send him an e-mail before first period.

But where should they meet? Copperchino? Misty Falls? She let her mind zip through the options. Every place she put him inside her mind, she saw him kicking back while she drew. When she walked into the library, she knew where she'd tell him to meet her. It was time.

● ● ●

"So what happened?"

Jacie startled, hitting SEND before she turned to face Solana.

"It was a conference," Jacie said.

"Liar," Solana said, pulling up a chair to sit next to her. "You've done something to disrupt the whole group."

Jacie looked in her lap.

"You think I care the group is disrupted?" Solana asked.

"You sound like it."

"No. I'm just wondering what happened. Whatever it was, Tyler is looking like a confused puppy, wondering which friend he should stand for—you, Becca, or Hannah. Becca looks ticked. Hannah looks upset."

"Hannah has every right to be upset." Jacie played with the mouse, clicking on this and that without really paying attention to what she was doing. She opened and closed options.

Solana lost some of her bluster. "So what happened?" she asked softly. She leaned forward. "Alyeria," she said.

The name of the group's childhood hideaway meant safety and sisterhood. It was where they'd come to love each other—before *Brio*.

Jacie nodded, tears coming to her eyes. "I blew it, Sol. I know you don't think much about our beliefs in God and stuff, but you know how important it is to me." She looked up at Solana.

Solana nodded. "I'll shut up and be a good friend and just listen."

"Is it okay if I don't talk about it?"

"Of course," Solana said, pulling Jacie's head to her shoulder. She stroked her hair a moment. "Is it that guy?"

Jacie jerked her head up, alarmed. "What guy?"

"The one you won't tell us about. The one you just e-mailed."

Jacie's shoulders sagged. She shook her head.

"Is he nice?" Solana asked.

"I can't talk about him."

Solana smiled. "You can't talk about anything, can you?" She poked Jacie. "Come on. We need to get to first period."

"You won't tell?"

"Alyeria, remember?"

Jacie knew she would keep quiet. The little Solana had guessed would not be repeated or discussed among the others. Long ago, in Alyeria, the four of them had promised to always keep secret everything that was spoken of in their hideaway.

Solana gave Jacie a quick hug. "Whatever happened yesterday, I'm sure the God you believe in is big enough to forgive it—even if it was the horrible thing you think it was. I have a feeling it wasn't so bad."

"It was," Jacie said.

Lunch didn't go well. Jacie didn't want to be there, but decided she should. Hannah sighed often, but otherwise kept quiet. Becca poked at her salad and burger, taking bites, then grumbling, then being quiet again.

Solana and Tyler tried to get the morose group to cheer up. Tyler threw ketchup-tipped fries at Solana, and she deflected them with a burger bun.

Hannah's disappointment soaked into Jacie. She took it as something direct from God Himself. After all, wasn't Hannah more in tune with God than any of them would ever be? Her whole life seemed so connected with God and Scripture that she was miles ahead of Jacie—who lately hadn't even been picking up her Bible to read a verse, much less have a quiet time with God. Jacie hadn't quit praying, but she figured that didn't amount to much in the scheme of things.

"Oh, Solana," Tyler said, changing to a serious tone. "I heard something about animal testing that I think you'd really like."

"Oh, please," Becca protested. "Not something else controversial to throw into this group. We've had enough commotion as it is."

"Really?" Solana said, leaning forward. She almost dipped her front into her own puddle of ketchup.

"Yeah, it's from somebody named Fry and Laurie," Tyler continued. "Have you heard of them?"

"No," Solana said.

"They said, 'I think animal testing is a terrible idea.'"

"They've got that right," Solana agreed.

"Yeah, they're against it because 'the animals get all nervous and give the wrong answers.'"

Solana threw her head back and laughed. Becca smiled. Jacie

snickered. Hannah's face didn't change at all.

The bell rang. "See you after?" Solana asked Jacie as she gathered her lunch trash and backpack.

"No. I think I have things to do," Jacie said.

"What kind of things?" Solana pressured.

Jacie shrugged. "Just stuff."

"I hope you're going to the studio to draw," Becca said, gathering her own lunch trash and backpack.

"Yeah," Jacie said. Something inside her stirred—the same thing she'd felt at the conference. She not only *wanted* to go draw, she *had* to. It was almost like a compulsion. She was being pulled toward her studio, compelled to take all that had happened and put it to paper, as if drawing would suck out of her what felt like poison.

chapter 17

Precisely at 8:00 that night, a motorcycle churning up dust came slowly down the lane. She opened the door to her studio, her eyes and smile welcoming him.

"Wow, this is great," Damien said as he stepped through the door. He stood there, taking in everything around him as though it were a grand home. His green eyes sparkled in fascination. "You really *are* an artist."

"What did you expect?" Jacie asked, teasing.

"I guess I expected something neat. A small sketchbook, maybe. But not this!" He waved his arm toward the stacks of canvases leaning against each other on the floor, the watercolors tacked all over the walls, the discarded sketches littering the floor.

He picked up the alarm clock and set it down, then picked up her stack of CDs and looked at the titles. "You aren't a very modern girl, are you?"

"Not when I'm painting. All my more socially acceptable CDs are at home."

"And what are they?"

"A confusing collection of alternative, R & B, adult contemporary, Christian. Anything else that strikes my fancy . . . Celtic . . ."

"You sound like a very mixed-up girl."

She plopped into her chair. "You've got that right." She didn't like that he accidentally got right to the truth of something she wanted to pretend wasn't there.

"I didn't mean it like that." He sat on the ottoman and leaned forward to look into her face.

"I know you didn't."

"What's wrong?"

"Nothing, really."

"You don't lie very well, do you, Jacie?"

She shook her head. He took her hands in his own. His thumbs rubbed hers. She hated that a tender touch from him could melt her completely.

"Do you want to talk about it?"

She shook her head.

"Okay!" he said brightly. He picked up some of her sketches, flipped through them, then put them on the table. He got almost a little-boy look on his face. "Would you draw me?" he asked shyly, not looking at her.

Jacie felt her insides skip. She couldn't tell him she'd tried—and failed to draw his eyes.

"I bet everyone asks you to draw a picture of them."

"Yeah, they do," Jacie said without getting up to gather her drawing things. She didn't know if she wanted to draw him or not. She was afraid to. There was something very personal about drawing someone in their presence.

"Should I have not asked?"

"I make funny faces when I draw," she blurted.

"You'd make me look like a clown?"

"No!" she laughed. "I mean I do funny things with my own face when I draw."

"What if I promise not to laugh?"

Jacie looked at her sketchbook on the table. She glanced at the charcoal pencil next to it. "Why do you think people always want me to draw them?" she asked.

Damien slid to the floor, leaning against the table leg, and folded his arms behind his head. He cranked his head back to look up at her. "Do you think it makes them feel more real?"

Jacie tilted her head, questioning.

"I mean, if someone can capture the real you on paper, maybe you really exist."

Jacie felt like he'd slugged her with truth. "What about photographs?" she asked.

"Big deal. So someone pointed a camera at you and clicked a button. A good drawing means someone could truly see inside you and put you down on paper or canvas. I think a portrait is a lot more revealing than a photograph, don't you? Well, at least that's my dumb guy idea."

"It makes sense to me."

"Maybe it's kind of like a fictional story that can show more truth than nonfiction." He paused, then grinned a crooked smile. "At least that's what a cute girl who sniffs books once told me."

Jacie blushed and smiled. Suddenly, she knew she wanted to draw him. She wanted to make him real—for both of them.

She sat him in the chair, turning it so the fading light was on his face. She set the lamp in various places until she was pleased with the way it highlighted his features. She sat on the ottoman and looked at him, taking in the shape of his eyes, the shape of his head. She studied the hair against his scalp, and the hair that didn't lie down. She looked down his neck to his T-shirt, noticing for the first time that it was fraying a little. She took care to notice his ears and the curve and dips of them. Looking into his eyes, she tried to see beyond the color and shape. She held her charcoal pencil over the sketchpad and looked from him to the pad. Finally, her hand began to move.

Damien kept silent. He had a Mona Lisa smile on his lips. The more she drew, the more that hint of a smile made her bubble inside until she felt like laughing. She finished the sketch and flipped the page.

"Let me see."

"Not yet. I want to get something else."

"Like what?"

"I don't know. Just be quiet."

He made a face at her.

She laughed.

"Like that?" he asked.

"No, not like that." She started to draw again. She wasn't sure what she wanted to capture, either. She'd know it when she saw it. Or when she'd drawn it.

He kicked back in the chair. "You never told me about your weekend."

"I didn't think you'd want to know—all that Christian stuff you don't like." She outlined the basic shape of his head.

He shrugged. "I still want to know how it was for you."

She put down her pad. *Okay. Here's my chance to tell him everything I learned. To tell him how much Jesus loves him and tell him about salvation and witnessing.*

"We learned a lot," she started lamely.

"Was it boring?"

"Not at all! It was awesome to be with so many kids who all believe the same thing. They had great music. I loved the speakers. They were so funny and gave lots of good information."

"So why did you come back all sad?"

"I didn't."

Damien just looked at her.

She looked down at the pad and started to fiddle with the corners of the pages. "I messed it all up. I tried, but I did it all wrong."

"How can you mess up going to a conference? All you do is sit and listen and yell and meet new people and have fun."

Jacie doodled on her pad. She couldn't look at him. "That wasn't the point of this conference."

"What was the point?"

Jacie sighed and drew a quick sketch of the old couple from the mall. "The point was for me to learn how to share my faith."

Silence.

Damien's voice sounded hard. "To try and convince me and everyone else that we're bad. Doomed to hell. Sinners. Lost."

"Not you," she said. But yes, him. *Them!* she wanted to say about the people on her paper. She looked at him. "Not to convince everyone that they're bad, either. But yes, that all of us are messed up and can't make it to God by our own efforts."

He stood and walked across the room, now only lit by yellow lamplight. "So what went wrong?"

Jacie couldn't tell if that was sarcasm in his voice. "Everything," she said. "I couldn't do it. I had the perfect chance, and I couldn't think of the words. All the things I know suddenly sounded stupid and awkward and what is real to me suddenly disappeared from my head."

Damien didn't move. He said nothing. He stood, staring out the window into the darkness.

"I'm such a failure as a Christian. I can't even tell someone about God. And I'm supposed to. If I don't, then I really don't believe what I say I believe, do I?" Jacie bit her bottom lip, trying to keep the tears away. "And I must not really care about other people enough. I'm just selfish. I'm stupid."

"Maybe the things you *believe* are stupid." Damien offered, his voice hard. "Have they really worked for anyone?"

"Yes!" Jacie said. "They've worked for me."

"All the time?" Damien challenged.

Jacie hung her head. "No. Not all the time. I don't understand God. Sometimes He seems so close and right there and sometimes He seems to have gone on vacation and forgot to leave His cell phone number."

"So why do you believe this stuff?"

Jacie sighed. "It's so hard to explain. But it *is* real. Because it makes sense. Because even when it doesn't make sense, it's real. Because some things in my life only make sense if God is in the picture. Because there are miracles that don't make sense and can only be explained with God's hand in them."

"And when God doesn't do miracles?" Damien asked, his voice taking on a ragged edge.

"You see? That's what I don't get. Why the Bible says that God wants everyone to be saved, and God wants us to help out, and then when I try and I can't do it, since God is perfect, there must be something wrong with *me*." Jacie threw her charcoal pencil at the wall. "I can only think that God really hates me for not getting it. For not doing it right."

"No," came Damien's voice so soft, Jacie almost didn't hear it. "He hates *me*."

Jacie didn't know what to think or say. She'd been so involved in her own frustration and questions, she hadn't even wondered what Damien thought. She tried to clear her head and consider his words. She wanted him to talk more, but was afraid if she said anything he'd run away. On the other hand, if she didn't say anything, would he think she didn't care?

When Damien turned around, the pain in his eyes shocked her. "God doesn't hate you for such a stupid thing, Jacie. Don't you realize that?"

"God doesn't hate anybody," Jacie said just as quietly.

"You just said He hates *you*."

"I know. I think He's really mad at me, but I guess I don't think He really hates me."

"I *know* He hates me, Jacie." He turned back toward the window. He sucked in big chunks of air.

Jacie moved behind him. She put her head on his back and put her arms around his waist. He plucked them off and moved away. "You'll hate me too." His voice was shaky.

"Why do you think God hates you?"

"Because I killed a little boy." His words came out choppy.

Jacie thought her heart stopped. She stepped back, sitting hard in her chair. "That's why you're here?"

He turned around, anger on his face. "Yes. That's why I'm here. I killed a kid. No one wanted me around anymore. They didn't trust me."

Jacie swallowed. Fear prickled her spine. "How?"

Damien moved toward her. Jacie pressed herself back into the chair. He dropped to the floor and put his head into her lap. He started to sob.

She didn't know what to do. Was he a killer? Should she run to Russell's for help? She'd never been around any male who cried, much less who sobbed so hard. Her hand hovered over his head. Finally she set it softly on his hair and began to stroke, as her mother did when she was crying.

"I didn't mean to," the words came broken, between sobs. "I swear it was an accident."

God. You've really got to help me this time. What do I say?

Silence.

"I was driving up the hill toward home. The sun was setting and blinding me. And then, out of nowhere, this kid is flying on his bike . . . and . . . and . . . I *hit* him."

The sobs came harder. Jacie said nothing, but continued to stroke his hair. Her heart felt sick.

"I can still see his face, Jacie. I can see the scared look just before he hit the windshield. Oh, God, I can still see his face."

Jacie could not imagine. Not in a million years. Tears started to drip down her own cheeks. "I'm so sorry," she whispered.

"That's why I can't drive a car. I'm so scared of it happening again."

"I wouldn't want to, either," she said, shivering.

"He didn't die right then," Damien continued. "He went to the hospital. I prayed and prayed and prayed. I *begged* God to save him. I begged God. I told God I'd stop being a screw-up. I told God I'd pay attention in youth group and stop going just because my parents made me. I told God I'd finally get serious about being a Christian."

Jacie stopped stroking his hair. She stared down at him. *He's a Christian? He's been one all along?* She wanted to ponder that, be so happy about that. *Then he can be mine, right? That means we can really be boyfriend/girlfriend, right?*

Damien started talking again. "I prayed so much, Jacie. Isn't God supposed to answer prayers?"

Jacie nodded dumbly, knowing he wasn't really looking for a spoken answer.

"I prayed nonstop for three days until that kid died. I even prayed *after* he died. I prayed maybe that he'd be raised from the dead. But nothing happened. My prayers got stuck in the sky. They left my mouth. They left my brain. They left me, but either they never got to God, or God ignored them."

Jacie covered her face. Her own tears came faster. She wanted to give Damien something. *Something* from God. Something that would help him see that God didn't hate him. Words from the Bible that would make him feel better.

God? Give me the verses I know. Please. PLEASE. She started to feel frantic. No words were coming. No verses. Nothing. She bent over and put her cheek on his. Her tears mixed with his. She opened her mouth several times, hoping that if she opened it, the right words would come out.

The verse that *did* come to her brain was from Luke. Something about the Holy Spirit giving you the words at that moment. But those were the only words that went through her head. "How awful," she whispered. "I'm so sorry. I'm so sorry."

She wished she could give a piece of her heart to him, as if that would comfort him. She wanted to give him something of herself to give him strength. All she could do was blubber with him. All she could do was give him a kiss on the cheek and tell him, "I don't hate you."

Her alarm clock went off, startling them both. He jumped up, wiping his face with his fists. "Don't tell anyone what I've told you." He looked embarrassed. "I'm sorry I even told you. No one knows. No one should ever know."

He ran out the door. A second later the motor flared and he was gone.

Gone for good, Jacie thought. Her heart ached—for him, for the little boy, for herself.

chapter 18

It chewed on her all week. It gnawed at her, a tiny mouse nibbling and nibbling. Why couldn't she do it? Why couldn't she build a bridge from Damien to God?

It seemed there would be no more chances. She'd see him at school, his face locked into the hard, keep-away-from-me look that he'd had when she first saw him. If she and he were in the same hallway, he'd turn and walk away.

She avoided her studio the rest of the week. She cried herself to sleep every night. She picked up her Bible and opened it to the Psalms and stared at the words. She might as well have been trying to read it in the original Hebrew.

She tried to pray for Damien, but didn't know what to say except, *God, help him. Somehow help him*. She did her homework. She watched sitcoms. She put on her Christian face and did a good job of pretending in front of her friends. She smiled at Hannah and told her she was working with the Lord on her flaws—which she hoped was not a lie.

Her prayers never stopped. *Oh God, Oh God. HELP! What's wrong with me? Fix me. Make me who You want me to be.* But her prayers felt stuck. Maybe they were stuck with Damien's. Were their prayers frolicking about, forgetting where they were supposed to be headed? Or was there some sort of shield that prevented the prayers of the imperfect from reaching God? Maybe He was too busy, or too annoyed by her lack of a quiet, daily alone time with Him. He was waiting, she was sure of it, until Jacie got everything in order before He answered her prayers.

When you start having a productive quiet time for at least a month, then I'll listen, Jacie imagined Him saying.

When Damien comes back to Me as a direct result of your witness, then I'll listen.

When you repent of liking his kisses, then I'll listen.

Or maybe it was more basic than that: *When you repent of liking him, then I'll listen.*

"Jace? Are you okay?" her mother asked one evening, standing behind Jacie as she vegged on the sofa. She gently stroked Jacie's hair. It made Jacie want to fall into her mother, laying her head on her mother's lap. But that would be too weird, too childish, too weak. *Actually, it would just remind me too much of Damien.*

"Hard week," Jacie said.

"Anything I can do?"

"No, thanks," Jacie said, trying to sound happy. It came out sounding too high.

"If you want to talk . . ."

"I know," Jacie said. "Thanks."

Friday afternoon, Jacie told her friends she wouldn't be there that night for their weekly get-together. "I've got other plans," she told them.

"Like what?" Becca asked. "This is like church. You don't miss unless you have a really good excuse."

"I have other plans."

Solana raised an eyebrow at her. Jacie gently shook her head.

"We were going to play basketball," Becca said with a glint in her eye.

"Only after rock climbing at the gym," Tyler said.

"Oh, Jock Night in Copper Ridge," Jacie said sarcastically. "My favorite."

"You like it okay," Becca protested.

"Sometimes," Jacie said.

"I can't go," Hannah told them without being asked.

"Would you want to?" Solana asked.

"I've never been rock climbing," Hannah told them.

"I could teach you," Tyler said. "It really isn't all that scary—lots of harnesses and things—"

"To keep you from crashing to the boulders below," Becca added.

Tyler threw her a look.

"I can't go because we're having Family Night," Hannah said.

"I thought that was Wednesday nights," Tyler said.

The girls looked at each other. "He knows her schedule?" Becca asked.

"Why not?" Solana said. All three broke into laughter.

"We had to postpone it," Hannah said.

"Bye," Jacie said, waving and walking away without turning to answer their cries of protest. She didn't want them to pry out the truth that her plans were to be alone. Her mother was going to the theater with friends and would think Jacie was going to be at Becca's as usual. A perfect time for Jacie to—do what?

She didn't know then, and she didn't know all that evening as she paced. She cleaned her bathroom. She cleaned her bedroom. She vacuumed the whole townhouse. She stared out the window, wishing for snow, even though it was only late September. *It's possible, you know, God*, she said, as if He were laughing at her for even wishing.

● ● ●

When she woke Saturday morning, there was only one thing she could do. "Mom, I'm going to the studio. I don't know when I'll be back."

"Promise me you'll come tell me before you go anywhere else."

"I will."

"Will you be gone all day?"

"I might," Jacie said, throwing an apple, some Chips Ahoy! cookies, and a peanut butter and jelly sandwich into a bag. As an afterthought, she tossed in three Capri Suns.

Jacie opened the door to her studio and pushed aside old frames and canvases of partially painted scenes to find a blank canvas she'd hidden. She'd kept it out of sight, not wanting to remind herself of the block that kept her from using it. She set it on an easel and got out her acrylics. If she was careful, she could do it. She'd learned the technique. She'd tried it before and was pretty good at it.

She took out the brush and opened the Bone Black and the Alizarin Brown. She was glad that sometime during the summer she'd already primed the canvas by covering it with a coat of White. It was ready to go.

She laid out an array of brushes as if she were a surgeon ready to cut open the patient. In some ways, that's what she was about to do. Only the surgery would be on herself.

She took her #8 shader brush and lifted it. She daubed it into the black and began, her mind and heart working together. The strokes came quickly and surely. For a moment she was aware of the speed at which she painted, and that she hadn't painted this quickly since— well, she couldn't remember. It didn't matter. The story took over. The piece of her soul that wanted to come out moved miraculously from inside her to the brush to the canvas.

She opened more colors. She mixed, she stroked, she daubed. She moved with long strokes, then short ones.

She listened to music, changing the CDs when she needed different music for different parts of the painting. Andreas Vollenweider, George Winston, *Rhythm of Creation*, James Galway playing Mozart on his flute. She moved and flowed with the music, knowing precisely which music she needed to ease the work inside her to become the work on canvas. It was like giving birth. The art was inside, waiting to be born. And like some babies, it needed help to emerge into the world outside. Music, for her, helped this to happen.

Her heart seemed to be whispering a prayer. For the first time in months, she sensed some sort of connection with God. She felt His presence in her heart, in her spirit, in her mind. He was silent, but He was there. All her words of faith that had been hiding in some secret room inside her flowed out. They danced, they played, they talked. They told of God's love and faithfulness in the hard times. They told of His generous kindness. The generosity that loved and saved anyway—in spite of what she'd done wrong or stupid or by accident or on purpose—as long as she admitted it and asked for God's help.

The words came and she painted.

A few times she stood, stretched her legs, and ate something. She walked around the canvas, looking at it, drinking it in. Then she would sit down again and paint some more. She turned the easel and her painting chair so the sun was always behind her. She painted without thinking, but with feeling. Sometimes an ache swelled inside. Sometimes tears poured down her face. Sometimes she gritted her teeth, determined. And sometimes she felt something let loose and spill through her.

Then, with more done on the painting than she could have expected, she wondered why she was having trouble seeing. She looked up. It was dusk.

She turned on her light and set the alarm for an hour before her curfew. She didn't want her mother to come looking for her and see the painting. No one must see the painting. It was for her alone. It was her soul, her pain, her failure, her desire. It was all she wanted to be and couldn't; it was what she lacked. It was what she wanted to give of God to Damien's pain and couldn't—because it was too late.

When the alarm screamed, she cleaned her brushes. She put away her paints. She put the nearly-done painting in a corner to safely dry. She turned off the light and closed and locked the door.

She stepped into her car feeling oddly whole.

● ● ●

"Where have you been all day?" Becca demanded on the phone.
"Working," Jacie told her.

"Not at Raggs."

"No."

"At the studio?" Becca's voice sounded excited. "Did you work on your entry?"

"No," Jacie said.

"When are you going to do that?"

"Don't bug me, Becca."

"I'm only trying to be a good friend," Becca told her. "I only want you to go to the conference."

"Okay. I promise I'll finish my work this week."

Jacie hung up the phone. She felt as if she'd been in another world and was being pulled back to this one. It wasn't unusual for her to feel this way when a project was going well. It felt strange—and good at the same time.

"Your friends have been calling you all day," her mother said. "They've been worried about you."

Jacie nodded, taking the Trix cereal box from the cupboard. She opened it and began taking handfuls and stuffing them into her mouth.

"Becca told me what happened."

Jacie didn't say anything. The feelings of inadequacy came flooding back.

"I'm not sure we're all made the same," her mother said. "I think maybe God knows this. And maybe one day you'll be able to share like others. And maybe you never will."

"And if I never can, then what?"

Her mother looked her in the eyes. "God looks at our hearts, Jacie. At our intentions. God will use you if you want. Just not always in the way you expect."

"But it's all going wrong," Jacie told her. "I can't do it. I can't be who God wants me to be."

"Sometimes it seems all wrong at the time. And sometimes it *is* wrong. I personally am so grateful that God takes us from where we are. As long as we put our hand in His and let Him lead us, He will."

"Like you and Dad?"

Her mother pressed her lips into a thin line. "Yes, like me and your dad. What we did was wrong, but God has blessed us anyway."

"How?"

Her mother smiled and pulled her close. "I have you!"

"I'm not such a blessing."

Tears popped into her mother's eyes. "Oh, but you are!"

"Think of the life you could have had without me."

"I don't think of that because I can't imagine life without you. You have been my greatest joy. And I will miss you so much when you go off to college."

"But I'm a pain."

Her mother grinned. "Yeah, sometimes you are. Like when you were four and ate all my See's candy, had chocolate around your mouth, and said you didn't touch it."

"I didn't *touch* it," Jacie teased. "I *ate* it."

Her mother smacked her playfully on her arm. "But you see? By eating the candy you saved me from gaining five pounds."

They both laughed. They hugged. "Whatever it is you're working so hard on in the studio, keep at it."

"Can I go to the studio after church tomorrow?"

"No lunch together?"

"After lunch."

"No watching old movies on TV?"

Jacie raised her eyebrows.

"Of course, silly. You haven't been able to paint for so long. Whatever this is, you keep at it. Do your best."

chapter 19

On Sunday Jacie painted with as much passion as she had the day before. In church, she hadn't even listened. Her thoughts had been on what else needed to be part of the painting. Even her prayers had been for the painting. She didn't think God would answer, but it felt right to talk to Him about it. On her sermon notes she drew sketches of ideas, scribbled over them, then sketched some more.

In the studio she painted without stopping. Normally she would pace for a long time, then sit and paint a little only to pace again. This time she paced for a moment and sat and painted for a long time. She stood close and peered at the canvas. She stood far away and squinted at it. She adjusted, dabbed, painted over.

When her alarm went off, she had already cleaned her brushes. She was done. She couldn't believe it; usually, a canvas like that would take weeks to finish. But this had flowed so quickly, her hands moving so perfectly. It was complete.

She stood back to admire her work. No one would ever see it. No one ever *could* see it. It was the best thing she'd ever done, but she'd never be able to show it to anyone.

Still, that didn't make her sad. This painting was her cry to God, her heart's work, her silent voice finally speaking the truth. It was okay that it was just between God and her.

Finishing the painting seemed to unlock something inside her. The next morning she started drawing one picture after another. In class she drew instead of taking notes. As the week progressed, she completed the charcoal of the *puro tesoros* to Solana's delight. She drew portraits of small children playing in a park. She drew Becca's foster brother, Alvaro, holding his Cheerios box. She drew Alvaro in his pajamas riding his bicycle. She painted a watercolor of the falls in spring from a photo. She attempted watercolors of columbine flowers and managed to be fairly pleased with a couple.

"Can I please see?" Hannah asked, looking over Jacie's shoulder at lunch one day.

"No," Becca said, putting her hand gently on Hannah's shoulder. "We learned a long time ago that Jacie does much better if no one's watching. She'll show us when she's ready."

Jacie looked up at Hannah. "I'll take you to my studio one day," she said, feeling suddenly not so shy about someone seeing her work.

"Wow. Thanks," Hannah said.

Her drawing was going really well. But her heart was not. Her heart ached for Damien. She thought about him, prayed for him, missed him. Around her friends she pretended everything was all right. Every once in a while, Solana would tilt her head and look at her. "You okay?"

Jacie would force a smile and say, "I'm drawing like crazy. Why wouldn't I be okay?"

Solana looked at her more intently, her chocolate brown eyes narrowing the same way they did when she was involved in some science experiment.

On Wednesday the whole crew showed up at the studio, Hannah in tow.

"The deadline for entries is Thursday noon," Becca reminded her.

"We wanted to make sure you had something ready."

Hannah stood in the doorway, taking it all in. "Wow," she said over and over. "This is incredible."

"Get over it," Solana told her.

Hannah moved through the room as though she were on holy ground. Her mouth hung slightly agape, her hands clasped tightly, as if to keep them from touching anything. She circled the room slowly, staring at all the paintings, drawings, and artistic tools. "Wow," she repeated softly.

"Mom has promised to take my entries in for me," Jacie said. "But they're at home, so you can't see them."

Solana narrowed her eyes. "We can if we go over to your house."

"Mom's at work, and—"

"We know the rules," Becca said, sighing. "No one at your house when Mom's not home."

"Right."

"We just want to make sure you don't flake out on us."

"I'm not flaking," Jacie said. "Really."

Tyler rocked in the chair, flipping through a sketchbook. He picked up a pencil and started to draw. "Maybe I can submit something." The girls gathered around him, peering over his shoulder. "No!" he said, hiding the picture. In a high voice, a bad imitation of Jacie, he said, "I freeze up when people watch me draw."

Jacie playfully smacked him in the head. She turned around and saw Hannah tipping the private canvas toward her, trying to peer at it. "No!" Jacie said sharply. "That one is nobody's business."

"I'm sorry," Hannah said, gently letting it go back to its original place. "It looks like it's really good, though."

"How can you tell upside down and backwards?" Jacie said, hoping to deflect attention from anything she might have seen.

"Is it finished?"

"Maybe."

"I'm finished!" Tyler shouted. He held the sketchpad up over his head, so the girls could stand behind him and see.

"Well, isn't that a perfect self-portrait," Becca said with a snort.

"Naw, it's cuter than Tyler," Solana teased. "Way cuter."

Tyler tried to whack her with the sketchpad, but missed.

"Oh!" Hannah cooed. "You know how to draw Snoopy? Can you teach me?"

"Sure," Tyler said. "Come over here and sit at my feet like a good woman."

Solana bonked Tyler on the head. Becca slugged his arm. Hannah smiled and said, "Of course," totally missing the joke.

● ● ●

"That girl scares me," Solana said later at Copperchino, as she, Jacie, and Becca downed their favorite hot drinks. "Are men, like, what—kings or something?"

"Your dad is the king of *your* house," Becca reminded her.

"But that's because he's from the dark ages—the '50s. Or from the Latino culture. Not from America in the twenty-first century."

"Hannah *is* from a different culture," Becca reminded her. "Maybe she and Alvaro will run off somewhere together."

Jacie wiped latte foam off her top lip. "She's not so bad."

"Maybe not in *her* culture," Solana said. Her head turned as she watched a cute guy walk past. She winked at him when he looked her way.

Becca sighed. "I guess not. But I do get tired of her and Alvaro and their weird ways."

"Be nice, you guys," Jacie said. "So Hannah's been raised more conservative than we have. There's nothing wrong with that. It's just different. Both Hannah and Alvaro have to adjust to new things. You guys want people to accept you and your quirks. Why can't you accept them?"

Becca looked at her watch. "Oh great. Coach is going to kill me."

"Yeah, right," Solana said. "You just want to escape the Jacie lecture."

"It's not like I haven't heard it a million times before." Becca tossed her cup in a trash can and came back. She kissed her fingers and tapped Jacie on her head with them. "We love you anyway, Jace. You just keep reminding us, okay?"

Solana snorted. "Do we have to listen?" Then she smiled broadly. "Just teasing, Jace."

The moment Becca left, Solana turned to Jacie. "So, how's it goin'?"

Jacie tensed. "Fine."

"Really."

"Really. Fine."

Solana's eyes narrowed again. "I know that look, Jacie. I've had it too many times to not know it well."

"What look?" Jacie asked, immediately sipping her mocha latte to hide whatever it was Solana could see.

"The look of missing a guy. Of wishing he was there. I can see it in your eyes. In the fake way you try to make all of us think everything is okay."

Solana's insight took Jacie by surprise. She felt a clench of her heart and a throb in her throat that warned the arrival of tears was imminent.

"Why won't you talk about him?"

"I can't." The words escaped Jacie like a small rush of wind.

Solana's eyes narrowed even more. "Was he mean to you? Did he hurt you?"

Jacie smiled. "No, Sol."

"He's hurting you now."

Jacie shrugged. "I guess it can't really be helped."

Solana shook her head. "Distance will do that. I really wish you hadn't decided on a long-distance relationship. They're impossibly hard."

The mysterious guy in California, Jacie thought. The one who didn't exist. Solana thought he was making her so sad. Jacie didn't correct her.

Over the next few days, Jacie couldn't seem to decide what to stress over next. Her mind jumped from one worry to another, then back again, often in the middle of a thought. She'd worry about how

Damien was doing, which would make her think of the painting. That would make her think of the art contest, which would trigger worries about the two drawings she'd entered. Then she'd miss Damien because they'd planned to go to the contest together—which would make her worry about him again.

She was so absentminded, twice she found she'd forgotten to lock her shack and three times she'd returned to her car and found she'd forgotten to set the emergency brake. Fortunately, her friends were satisfied to blame her stress on the upcoming art show.

As far as Jacie was concerned, the sooner Saturday came and went, the better.

chapter 20

When the day finally arrived, Jacie didn't feel apprehensive anymore. She didn't want to admit it, but she was so excited she could have turned cartwheels.

She didn't know what to do with her hands. She shoved them into her coat pockets. She took them out and grasped them, wringing them a little the way she'd seen Gran do when she watched disturbing news items on TV. She bit her bottom lip and chewed on it a little. She kept trying to push curls back from her face, but her hair was already held back with clips.

As she and her friends passed each division, Jacie looked at the art that had won, the art that had not. She couldn't really focus on any of it, though, until she'd seen her own work.

"Who cares about this garbage?" Solana asked. "Let's go to where the real art is."

"But I want to see it all," Becca said.

"You do not," Solana said. "You don't even know what good art looks like."

"I do too," Becca said. She paused. "Well, I know what I like."

Hannah looked around as if searching for someone or something. Tyler stayed by her side, looking in the directions she did.

"Let's go see the charcoal stuff first," Solana said. "I want to know how much money Jacie won."

"Maybe I didn't win anything," Jacie said, trying to keep her hopes from getting too high.

"I bet you won," Hannah said. "You are too good not to have won." She smiled a little too broadly. Jacie was too nervous to wonder for long at what that smile meant.

Her stomach fluttered as the group headed toward the charcoal sketch division. She was afraid to hope.

Tyler gave her a quick rub on her shoulder.

Solana nudged her.

Becca, no longer pretending to care about *all* the art, marched forward.

Jacie held back, not wanting to know first.

"I want to see the acrylic paintings," Hannah said eagerly.

"Not yet," Solana hissed. "We're busy here."

Becca squealed. She pointed at a bright yellow ribbon on a charcoal sketch of wild horses running through a stream.

Solana beamed. "See? I told you the *puro tesoros* would be perfect subjects. How could they *not* win a prize?"

Jacie hugged herself, taking in the drawing and the ribbon together. "I won," she said, disbelieving.

"Of course you won!" Solana said.

"I'm so happy for you," Becca said, giving Jacie a hug. "I bet this feels like when our volleyball team won the regionals, huh?"

"So, how much did you win?" Tyler asked.

"I think I won $100," Jacie said. She was glad she'd won the prize, but sad that it wasn't enough to put a dent in what she needed for the National Art Conference.

"I guess I should have been more specific," she said.

"Excuse me?" Solana said.

"I told God that if I won, I'd go. But I didn't pray for a prize big enough to pay the way."

"So?" Becca asked. "Are you going or not?"

Jacie nodded. "I guess, but I don't know how. I suppose I'll have to trust God."

"Oh, He'll provide," Hannah said. "Trust me."

Solana rolled her eyes.

Jacie wanted Hannah to be right. But she wasn't really sure God *would* provide.

"Let's look at all the entries!" Hannah said. "It'll be fun!"

Now Jacie could pay attention to the other entries and prizes. She took so long at each entry, her friends were getting impatient. Hannah kept going to the end of the aisle and looking ahead. Tyler would skim a row of entries, then stand to one side, watching people and tapping his foot. Finally he said, "Can you come back later and look some more, Jacie? I mean, get your hand stamped or something?"

Jacie laughed. "They don't stamp your hand at an art show. But yeah, I guess I can look later."

"I really want to look at the acrylics," Hannah said. "They're my favorite. Can we?"

"Fine," Becca said. "This is Jacie's show, but sure, we'll do whatever you want, Hannah."

"Of course," Tyler said. "Are they near the end?"

As they rounded the corner, Jacie froze. Halfway down the aisle, a guy squatted in front of a painting.

It was Damien.

"Come on," Hannah urged, tugging at Jacie's sleeve.

Jacie couldn't move. She hadn't been close to Damien since that night. She was sure he didn't ever want to see her again. She longed to be close to him—but not now, not with her unsuspecting friends surrounding her.

As Hannah tugged at her, Jacie stared at Damien. And Damien stared at the painting, engrossed. Maybe *disturbed* was more accurate. His jaw worked the same way it had when they'd confronted the cruel man and his dog on the trail.

People stopped behind Damien, looking at the painting and commenting. *They* looked pleased, Jacie thought. So what was with Damien?

Solana and Becca were discussing a portrait of a little girl hanging in front of them with a second place ribbon attached. "If this is *second* place, I wonder what would be *first*," Becca was saying. "It's awfully good."

Hannah was still tugging. Jacie pulled her arm away. *What should I do?* she thought. If she greeted Damien, her friends would know her secret. If she didn't, it might hurt his feelings even more. Quietly, so Damien wouldn't hear, she said, "Let's go over there," and pointed toward another aisle.

"Look!" Solana said loudly. "There's that guy who ran us off the road. Now's my chance to meet him! Do I look okay?" She adjusted her skirt and mushed her lips together to spread around whatever lipstick clung to them. She began strutting toward him.

Jacie felt sick, unable to move. She knew she should run. All she could do was swallow and feel a terror rising in her stomach.

Damien slowly turned his head. Solana raised her hand to start a friendly, flirty wave—the one Jacie had seen at least a hundred times. But as he stood, he looked straight at Jacie. Hurt and anger crossed his face.

Solana stopped. She pivoted on one sandaled foot to follow Damien's gaze.

Hannah marched forward toward the picture Damien had been absorbed in. "Come on, you guys, let's go down here."

Damien passed Solana, then passed Hannah. He stopped in front of Jacie. She looked into his eyes and felt the pain pour from them.

"How *could* you?" Damien asked. "I *trusted* you."

Jacie opened her mouth, but nothing came out. *What is he talking about?* she thought. Feeling the stares of her friends, she put her hand on his arm.

He yanked it away. "Don't touch me," he said. He gave her one last, hard look. "Don't *ever* touch me again," he added, walking briskly into the crowd.

Jacie turned to follow him. As she did, someone grabbed her arm. "Come *on*," Hannah was saying.

The others seemed stunned into silence. "Come on, everybody!" Hannah chirped. "You've got to see this."

Jacie let herself be dragged. She felt confused. Scared. Dead.

Hannah placed her in front of the painting Damien had been looking at. "There!" she said, obviously delighted.

Jacie focused on the painting. Instantly the sick feeling became an overwhelming wave of weakness. She put her hand to her mouth. "Oh, no," she whispered through her fingers.

"Isn't it *great?*" Hannah said, dancing from foot to foot. "Look! It's *incredible*."

"It's *him*," Solana said, looking at the painting, then toward the direction of Damien's retreat.

Becca stared at the painting, then at Jacie. "When?" Her voice was softer than cotton.

"Isn't anyone *happy?*" Hannah asked, her hands waving. "She got the *Grand Prize!* That's better than *First!*"

It was only then that Jacie noticed the Grand Prize ribbon attached like a purple chrysanthemum to the corner of the painting—*her* painting. The painting she did in secret, the outpouring of her heart. Her cry to God was laid open for the world to see.

For the third time in a few minutes it felt as though someone had punched her in the stomach. Only this time it was worse. Everything was laid bare—her relationship with Damien, Damien's secret, her heart. All with the world prancing by, pointing and making comments.

Jacie looked at the painting as if for the first time. In it, a broken Damien leaned back, his body slumping against Jacie, tears pouring from his wide, green eyes. Out of his opened hand, a tiny bicycle and boy fell toward the floor into an open grave. Jacie cradled him with her left arm, her head tilted to rest on his shoulder. Tears mixed with his, falling toward the grave. Her right hand was open before him, a sword and a cross as if ready to take.

She swallowed, knowing that all her friends were watching her.

"It's really, really, good," Becca said.

"The best you've ever done," Solana added.

Tyler only nodded.

Becca and Solana looked at each other, then at Jacie. "You caught his eyes this time," Solana said.

"Who did this?" Jacie asked, trying to hold back the rage in her voice.

Hannah's hand shot up, her smile lighting her face. "I did!"

"I can't believe you'd do this to me!" Jacie said. She ran down the aisle, dodging onlookers, her throat tight. As she ran, she kept seeing the look of betrayal on Damien's face.

In the parking lot she didn't think about what her friends would do for transportation if she drove off without them. She didn't care. She only wanted to get away fast.

When she threw the car into gear, it jerked backwards. Without looking for other cars, she zipped out of the parking lot and into the street. She barely noticed the trees and signs and buildings.

The parking lot at the elementary school was empty. She drove until her tires hit the curb of the sidewalk. She jumped out and ran, heading for her safe place—Alyeria.

Squeezing through the low bushes, she popped out into the clearing where a stand of aspens huddled together, their leaves a brilliant gold. A tiny breeze made the trees quake, their petal-shaped leaves shaking and twinkling in the setting sun.

As Jacie sat with her back against a white trunk, the tears began to flow. Her face fell to her knees, and she started to sob. Above her the aspens let loose their leaves, falling around her like golden tears.

chapter 21

He doesn't understand. But how will I make him understand? Say it was a mistake? Yeah, right. As if painting a picture can be a mistake. I obviously spent a lot of hours on this thing. That was no mistake, and he knows it. But how can I convince him that I didn't mean for it to be in the show? And why would he believe me?

She breathed fast and deep, the aspens still quaking around her. She swallowed again and again. She jabbed a stick into the ground, then dropped the stick and covered her eyes.

She shook on the outside and on the inside. She bit her lip so hard she could taste blood.

● ● ●

"I wanted to kick her where she sits," Solana said as she, Becca, and Tyler entered Alyeria.

Jacie looked up, tears streaming down her face.

Becca sat next to her and put her arm around her. "Hannah's really sorry."

Solana made a face. "Yeah. She's really sorry. So sorry she started crying." Solana sighed as if disappointed. "She meant it. I know she did. It saved her behind, I'll tell you that."

"Why didn't you tell us about him?" Becca said.

Jacie shrugged. "I liked him so much. And you would have told me it was wrong."

"Was it?" Becca asked.

Jacie shrugged again. "I don't know."

"Well, he's certainly hot," Solana said. "How long has this been going on?"

"The first day of school."

Tyler sat in the corner of Alyeria, silent and watching.

Becca gave Solana a dirty look. "This girl's hurting. Can't you just lay off the guys for a moment?"

Solana stuck her tongue out at Becca. "I was just trying to commiserate, okay?"

Jacie picked up a stick and began drawing in the dirt. "Damien told me some secrets about himself." Jacie bit her lip again, trying to find the words she wanted. "He was hurting so bad. I wanted to give him verses. Let him know how much God loves him. But nothing came."

"So you painted it," Becca said.

Jacie nodded. "I didn't want anyone to ever see it. I made a promise."

Solana jumped up, slamming her fist into her other hand. "Now I'm really going to give it to Hannah."

Jacie shook her head, the tears pouring down her face. "No. Stay out of it."

"You're not going to let her get away with it, are you?" Solana asked.

"I'm really mad right now and I don't know what I'll do. But I'll do it myself."

The friends sat in silence for some time, gathering close to Jacie, sometimes patting her on her knee or rubbing her back.

Tyler suddenly spoke up. "Can you do something for me?"

"What?" Jacie asked, still drawing pictures in the dirt with a pointed aspen branch.

"I want you to go back to the show tomorrow—"

"I don't care about the show anymore."

"Just go back and stand near your painting." He put up his hand to quiet her and she stopped her protest. "I want you to just stand nearby and listen to what the people are saying about it."

"I'm so embarrassed," she said. "It's like I'm naked in that painting. It's my failures right out there for everyone to see."

Becca and Solana sat cross-legged on the ground, listening. Becca asked softly, "What failures?"

"My failure to give Damien what he needed most."

Solana put up her hand. "Don't take this wrong. But maybe you did."

Jacie shook her head. "I'm not going back."

"Please do it for me," Tyler said. "No one will know it's your painting."

"But I'm in it!"

"But not your face."

Jacie drew in the dirt.

"Please?"

Jacie thought, remembering.

"We'll make a pact," they had said together in eighth grade. All of them. They would be friends forever. Trusting each other to want the best for one another. Encouraging each other to grow in their relationship with God.

Jacie looked up into Tyler's eyes. "Only for you."

● ● ●

Later that night Jacie could hear her mother answer the door. Voices grew louder as they moved down the hall and stood outside Jacie's bedroom.

Jacie didn't answer the knock, but the door opened anyway. "Someone is here to see you," her mother said. "I think you should talk."

Someone moved into the room, took Jacie's chair from her desk, and moved it next to the bed. Jacie lay still, her face to the wall.

"I'm so sorry," Hannah said, her voice sounding choked.

Jacie closed her eyes.

"I had no idea."

"You knew the rules," Jacie said.

"Yes, I did," Hannah said softly. "I was so wrong. I got carried away when I saw that picture. I thought for sure it would win and . . . well, I guess . . ."

Jacie sat up, turning to face Hannah. Hannah's eyes were red from crying. She shifted her gaze to stare at her hands.

"I really wanted to be your friend," Hannah continued. "I thought if I did something to help you, then you guys would accept me into your circle."

Jacie shook her head. "That backfired big time."

Hannah looked at Jacie. "It's one of the things I tend to do," she tried to explain. "I like to help people and sometimes I help where I shouldn't. My mom is always telling me I've got to stop butting in. Maybe it's because I'm taking care of my little sisters and brother so much . . ." her voice trailed.

"You hurt me," Jacie said. "But you hurt someone else even more."

"I know," Hannah said, tears trickling down her face. "I'm sure you can never forgive me, but I'm asking you to anyway."

Jacie swallowed. Nothing inside her wanted to forgive Hannah. But she knew God wanted her to. "I'll try," Jacie said. "I'll ask God to help me."

Hannah nodded. "My mom is waiting in the car."

She stood and left the room, closing the door gently behind her.

● ● ●

Jacie walked up and down the aisle at the art show, waiting for people to come by. She felt silly. Scared. She was afraid people would ridicule her work, the way Becca and Solana had done with others'.

She tried standing one aisle over. She could hear only snatches of the comments. So she moved back to the aisle where her art hung, pretending to look at the other paintings. Although she didn't look at the speakers, she heard everything.

"What do you think of this one?" a man said.

"Powerful," the woman answered. "Do you think she's trying to offer the grieving man something from God?"

"How horrible," someone else said. "Something must have happened with that bicycle boy. His brother, maybe?"

"A friend?"

"Maybe it's symbolic of himself."

An older woman stood toward the back, clutching her hands to her chest. "Faith is our only hope for such tragedies, isn't it?"

As Jacie listened, her heart jumped. She'd wanted to believe it, but had been afraid to even think it. *Could it be that* painting *is my witness? Could it be that my voice is* art?

The thought rushed over and through her. Maybe she could speak to others through what she loved and felt the most.

It was as if a door had opened in her head. She remembered music that made her think of God and want to be closer to Him. She thought of books, stories, articles, and poetry—words that were powerful and turned her heart toward God. Dance. Drama. *All* forms of art were ways God could show Himself to people, weren't they? Why not? And why not her paintings?

Her heart started beating faster.

"Nothing like yours, Dear, nothing like yours." A vaguely familiar voice drifted up the aisle.

"Oh, Henry, you always thought too highly of my work."

Jacie's eyes widened. "Doris! Henry!" she said.

"My, my, look what the cat drug in," Henry said, grinning.

"Do you have something entered?" Doris asked, looking about her.

Jacie hesitated, then pointed to her painting.

"Oh, Honey! This one? Look at that!" Doris said. "Best of Show for Acrylics! And well-deserved, too."

Jacie blushed.

"Look at her artistic eye," Henry said to Doris, bending over to examine the painting more closely. "She's captured it."

"Yes. It's very good."

"You didn't do many acrylics."

"No. I was better with watercolor."

"Always watercolor," Henry agreed.

Doris moved about, examining the painting from various distances. "This was a work of the heart," she said. She turned to Jacie. "Work like this shows genius."

"I don't think so, Doris," Jacie said.

"You will go far, Honey. I know you will."

Henry looked at the painting intently. "Doris knows what she's talking about. You'd better listen to her."

Doris tilted her head and looked at the painting again. "This is what you were trying to tell us at the mall, wasn't it, Dear?"

Jacie nodded.

"It looks as though the girl is trying to give the young man something he could use for his grief. Is that it?"

Jacie nodded again.

Doris looked at the painting a long time.

Jacie finally got up enough nerve to open her mouth. "I had all these words locked up inside. And this was the only way I could speak."

"Your voice is strong."

"And so is my faith."

Doris patted her arm. "I can see that."

"I'd like to get together with you sometime—and just talk. Would that be okay?"

"Why, we just might have to do that—Henry?"

"You always know what you're talking about. Well," he said, winking at Jacie. "Most of the time."

Jacie wrote her phone number on a piece of paper, which Henry stuffed into his pocket.

Doris pulled Jacie over and planted a kiss on her cheek. "I'm proud of you, Dear. You do whatever you must to continue painting."

Jacie hugged her back, and the old couple walked away.

She watched them go, until she sensed someone come up behind her.

Someone touched her hair softly, pulling it back from her face. She closed her eyes, instantly knowing who it was. But she was too afraid to look into those hurting, green eyes.

His hand took her arm and turned her toward him.

"Oh, Damien. I'm *so* sorry," she said, searching his eyes. "It wasn't supposed to be here. Someone entered it without me knowing. I know it's my fault for painting it. Maybe I had no business doing it, but I couldn't express what I felt and what you said—"

He put his finger against her lips. "It's okay."

"No, it isn't," she protested.

"It's not okay that the whole world knows or that the painting is here. But it's okay that you painted it. It's okay because now I see something." He paused and Jacie thought she'd lose herself in his silence. "Maybe God doesn't hate me as much as I thought."

Jacie looked at him quizzically, hopefully. She didn't dare let her excitement surface.

"It's the painting—your painting—that makes me understand ... something." He looked at his shoes, and took a deep breath. "Ever since ... the accident, I've felt a sort of ... oh, I don't know ... like God was tugging at me or something. Maybe He was trying to offer me a little help."

With his finger he brushed away a curl that had fallen into her face. "You never condemned me, Jacie. You never said I was a bad person." His voice dropped to a whisper. "You let me cry. You cried with me. You didn't make fun of me, and you didn't try to shove God at me. I never would have understood if you had."

"But I wanted to tell you that stuff so I could give you all the right answers."

Damien smiled. "Not everybody can hear it like that, Jace."

"But I didn't *do* anything."

"Yes, you did. You showed me God by listening. You painted this to help me understand."

She smiled weakly. "I painted this to help *me* understand."

"And now it's helping me, too."

"So are you okay with God now?" she asked, hoping.

"Of course not. But at least I'm thinking about Him now." He shook his head. "I even prayed last night, sort of. Right now it's mostly yelling and being mad. God probably wishes I'd just shut up again."

"No way," Jacie said. "As long as we're being honest with Him I think He's happy, since He already knows everything anyway."

He put his arm around her and kissed her on the top of her head. "Thanks, Jace." He pulled back and looked her in the eyes. "I missed you."

She melted again. "I missed you, too."

He looked around as if searching for someone. "Are your friends angry?" he asked.

"For what?"

"For you liking a bad boy."

"They were surprised. I suppose they were mad at first."

"Do you still like me?"

"Yes," she said breathlessly.

His eyes sparkled as he took her hand and walked her toward the exit.

"Can I still see you?" he asked.

"I want to more than anything." She stopped herself. "No," she said, surprised at what she was suddenly realizing. "What I want more than anything is to keep painting."

"You should."

"And I want to get back on track with God. I guess I've been afraid of Him lately."

Damien cocked his head, his eyes telling her to keep talking.

"I was afraid He'd make me dump you."

A tiny smile played on Damien's lips.

"But now," she said, looking at him intently, "I understand that He knows me so well that maybe I should trust Him more."

"Like how?"

"Like with the painting. And sharing my faith. I thought I wasn't any good at either one. And now I'm thinking that maybe I'm good at both—just not in the ways I thought I was."

He led her to a bench bathed in sunlight. He sat down; she sat next to him.

"So?" he asked. "Do we become an 'us'?"

She bit her lip and looked at the ground. She wanted to say yes so much. But she shook her head.

His face dropped. "Is it because of the accident?"

"No!" she said, looking into his face. "No, Damien. I really, really like you. But I need to get back on track with God and give Him my attention right now. As much as I want to, you're a distraction from that."

The crooked smile returned. "I guess you would be a distraction for me, too."

"But Damien . . . I want to be your friend. I want everyone to know that we're friends. I want you to come to our church if you want. I want to talk to you."

He nodded. "I guess I can live with that." He squeezed her hand. "See you, then?"

She squeezed back.

● ● ●

Jacie drove home, completely out of emotions. The past two days started to pour in on her. The award. Damien's shock. Amazement at what the painting had done for Doris and Henry. For Damien. For *herself.*

When she got home, she sat down at her desk. She dug the rumpled National Art Conference registration form from the bottom of her backpack and placed it in front of her. She smoothed it out. *No, I'm not like Hannah. God doesn't expect me to be like Hannah or anyone else.*

She smiled, took a pen and began to fill in the blanks—confidently, without hesitation.

FIND A FRIEND!

THE CHRISTY MILLER SERIES

Beginning with 14-year-old Christy Miller's commitment to Christ, this bestselling series follows her high school years as she grows in her faith. But as for every real-life teen, things are not always easy. She shares the same hopes, worries, and joys, and has to make the same tough choices that you do every day.

Author Robin Jones Gunn fills the books with stories on friendship, dating, responsibility, life at school, and sticking up for what's right—all the things that are most important to teens like you. Her beloved character Christy Miller has become a friend for over a million teens around the world and is ready to meet you today!

1. Summer Promise
2. A Whisper and a Wish
3. Yours Forever
4. Surprise Endings
5. Island Dreamer
6. A Heart Full of Hope
7. True Friends
8. Starry Night
9. Seventeen Wishes
10. A Time to Cherish
11. Sweet Dreams
12. A Promise Is Forever

CHRISTY AND TODD:
THE COLLEGE YEARS

1. Until Tomorrow
2. As You Wish
3. I Promise

◆BETHANYHOUSE

11400 Hampshire Ave. S. • Minneapolis, MN 55438 • 800-328-6109 • www.bethanyhouse.com

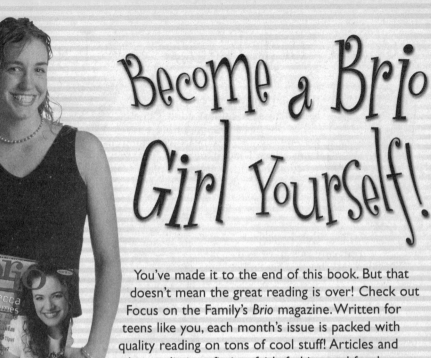

Become a Brio Girl Yourself!

You've made it to the end of this book. But that doesn't mean the great reading is over! Check out Focus on the Family's *Brio* magazine. Written for teens like you, each month's issue is packed with quality reading on tons of cool stuff! Articles and columns dig into fiction, faith, fashion and food ... and of course—guys! And it's all from a Christian perspective. Don't miss your chance to belong to an awesome group of *Brio* readers. Everyone's so close, they're like sisters.

Request a complimentary copy of this hot read *today* and become a *Brio* sis!

CALL Focus on the Family at 1-800-A-FAMILY (in Canada, call 1-800-661-9800)

LOG ON to www.briomag.org

OR WRITE to Focus on the Family, Colorado Springs, CO 80995 (in Canada, write P.O. Box 9800, Stn. Terminal, Vancouver, B.C. V6B 4G3)

Mention that you saw this offer in the back of this book.

For more information about Focus on the Family and what branches exist in various countries, dial up our Web site at www.family.org.

Check Out Focus on the Family's

The Christy Miller Series

Teens across the country adore Christy Miller! She has a passion for life, but goes through a ton of heart-wrenching circumstances. Though the series takes you to a fictional world, it gives you plenty of "food for thought" on how to handle tough issues as they come up in your own life!

The Nikki Sheridan Series

An adventurous spirit leads Nikki Sheridan, an attractive high school junior, into events and situations that will sweep you into her world and leave you begging for the next book in this captivating, six-book set!

Sierra Jensen Series

The best-selling author of The Christy Miller Series leads you through the adventures of Sierra Jensen as she faces the same issues that you do as a teen today. You'll devour every exciting story, and she'll inspire you to examine your own life and make a deeper commitment to Christ!

Mind Over Media:
The Power of Making Sound Entertainment Choices

You can't escape the ideas and images that come from the media, but you *can* weed through the bad and grasp the good! This video uses an exciting, MTV-style production to dissolve the misconceptions people have about the media. The companion book uses humor, questions, facts and stories to help you take charge of what enters your mind and then directs your actions.

Life on the Edge—Live!

This award-winning national radio call-in show gives teens like you something positive to tune in to every Saturday night. You'll get a chance to talk about the hottest issues of your generation—no topic is off-limits! See if it airs in your area by visiting us on the Web at www.lifeontheedgelive.com.

Cool Stuff on Hot Topics!

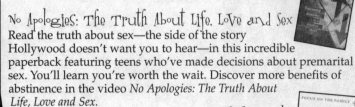

My Truth, Your Truth, Whose Truth?

Who's to say what's right and wrong? This book shatters the myth that everything is relative and shows you the truth about absolute truth! It *does* matter . . . and is found only in Christ! Understand more about this hot topic in the unique video *My Truth, Your Truth, Whose Truth?*

No Apologies: The Truth About Life, Love and Sex

Read the truth about sex—the side of the story Hollywood doesn't want you to hear—in this incredible paperback featuring teens who've made decisions about premarital sex. You'll learn you're worth the wait. Discover more benefits of abstinence in the video *No Apologies: The Truth About Life, Love and Sex.*

Masquerade

In this hard-hitting, 30-minute video, popular youth speaker Milton Creagh uses unrehearsed footage of hurting teens to "blow the cover" off any illusions that even casual drug use is OK.

The Ultimate Baby-sitter's Survival Guide

Want to become everyone's favorite baby-sitter? This book is packed with practical information. It also features an entire section of safe, creative and downright crazy indoor and outdoor activities that will keep kids challenged, entertained and away from the television.

Dare 2 Dig Deeper Girl's Package

Have you been looking for info on the issues you deal with? Yeah, that's what we thought. So we put some together for you from our popular Dare 2 Dig Deeper booklets with topics that are for girls only, such as: friendship, sexual abuse, eating disorders and purity. Set includes: *Beyond Appearances, A Crime of Force, Fantasy World, Forever, Friends, Hold On to Your Heart* and *What's the Alternative?*

**Visit us on the Web at
www.family.org or www.fotf.ca in Canada.**

PREFER TO USE A CREDIT CARD?

1-800-A-FAMILY
1 - 8 0 0 - 2 3 2 - 6 4 5 9

IN CANADA
1-800-661-9800
CALL US TOLL-FREE